Earth Sentinels: The Storm Creators

Praise for Earth Sentinels: The Storm Creators

———

"Quick paced with a powerful message."
— Greg Kincaid, *New York Times* Bestselling Author of
 A Dog Named Christmas

"This compelling adventure shows that our struggles around
the world are connected and that ordinary people have the
power to change the world for the better. I encourage all to
read *Earth Sentinels* and be inspired to take action."
— Dr. Margaret Flowers, PopularResistance.org and
 Co-chair of the Green Party

"A powerfully crafted story addressing the issues at the center
of our very survival as a species and sustainable civilization."
— WolfConnection.org

"Riveting! I found it difficult to put the book down. This
fiction reads as a non-fictional account of the spiritual side
of the indigenous people and the problems facing our world
today. A must read!"
— Dennis Nighthawk, healer and spiritual leader, retired
 military, and tribe member of the White Laurel Band of
 Cherokee

"*Earth Sentinels* is a well-crafted tale, instilling a powerful
message of hope for our planet."
— David Alfred Tetley, D.Min, author of *You Might Be a
 Christian, and Not Even Know It!*

"On occasion, we all read a book that we know will mark the time of our age. Where truth is illegal, communication is regulated and monitored, and humanity is impaled upon the skewer of power and greed, this book's message is every bit as telling and accurate as *Animal Farm* and *Fahrenheit 451*. It is a succulent portion of cold, hard truth played out with characters you share affinity with, understand and love."
— Mark Champion, OurHealingMatters.com

"Simply riveting! This book is a page turner to the end. Herrera has woven a cautionary tale with threads of history, revelation and hope. Bravo!"
— Richard O'Shields, Channel and Media Professional, www.EverydayConnection.me

"*Earth Sentinels* is a powerful read."
— Michael Wisotzke, Truth Seeker Forum

"The story opens doors for people on a spiritual journey. It's a book hard to put down!"
— Marie Savage, EarthWaterWellness.com

"Mother Earth is in danger, and Shaman Elizabeth Herrera points out exactly what humans are doing to her. This is definitely a recommended read."
— Lonny Hall, tribe member of Kon Kow Valley Band of Maidu, and grandson of Pamelo, Northern Maidu Shaman

A NOVEL

Earth Sentinels:
The Storm Creators

Book 1

Shaman Elizabeth Herrera

Earth Sentinels: The Storm Creators
Copyright © 2014, 2017 Shaman Elizabeth Herrera
Published by Blue Gator Inc.
All rights reserved.
Genre: Visionary Fiction, Contemporary Fantasy

ISBN-13: 978-0-9903492-4-2

A special thanks to my children,

Savannah and Zachary, who were

the catalysts for Earth Sentinels.

Janet Harvey-Clark: Your edits
made this story shine.

Renee Shaw: Your support has
been invaluable.

This book is dedicated to Jairo Mora, an environmental activist who was tortured and killed by turtle egg poachers. He had tirelessly campaigned and patrolled the beaches, protecting endangered sea turtles in Costa Rica.
He was only 26.

"Only after the last tree has been cut down, only after the last river has been poisoned, only after the last fish has been caught, only then will you find that money cannot be eaten."

— Cree Prophecy

Chapter 1

Bear Claw Lake

In a remote area of Canada, a white, double cab pickup truck sped down Highway 55 heading toward Bear Claw Lake, one of the deepest and largest bodies of water in the Alberta province, as well as the major tributary for the Saskatchewan and Beaver rivers. Traces of the Old North Trail ran beside its deep waters and through the surrounding dense forest, used for centuries by the Blackfoot Nation for migration and trading all the way from the permafrost Yukon Territory to sunny New Mexico. Inside the truck was a team of independent specialists commissioned by the Falicon Gas and Oil Company to investigate an ongoing oil spill.

The disaster had been caused by Falicon's use of the in-situ extraction method that pressurized the oil bed with extremely hot steam and chemicals, cracking the reservoir, causing the oil to escape through spider web ruptures in the earth.

The white pickup turned off the two-lane highway onto a dirt road, dust billowing as it sped toward the disaster. The driver wore a pistol strapped to his side and rested his arm on the console. A scientist sat in the front passenger's seat reviewing paperwork. He sighed, setting the papers down. The three engineers in the backseat rode quietly looking out the windows.

A glimpse of an old pickup in the rearview mirror caught the driver's attention. It was a 1973 two-tone Ford with a rusty chrome grill and bumper. Inside were two men from the nearby Bear Claw First Nation reservation. Tom Running Deer sat in the passenger seat holding a Winchester 30-30 rifle between his knees with the barrel protruding a few inches above the dashboard. His black t-shirt was taut over his muscular frame. A few gray hairs highlighted his long black hair that was held back in a ponytail. Beside him was his great-uncle, Chief Keme, who gripped the wheel with his strong hands. A sterling silver ring, accented with turquoise, decorated his right ring finger. He wore a clean, white shirt with a frayed collar. Both men fiercely glared at the intruders in front of them.

The company driver checked the rearview mirror again, saying, "Don't look, but we're being tailed by Indians." The engineers and scientist spun around, peering out the back window. "Jesus! I told you not to look!" The men quickly faced forward again. "Now keep your cool. They're probably just headed back to the rez, having a little fun with us." The driver's comments provided little relief to his nervous passengers.

The old Ford barreled in on the white pickup truck, nearly bumping its rear end before easing back. The engineers and scientist tensely waited for the driver to react, but he drove in silence until the Ford veered off, rumbling down another dirt road, disappearing behind a cloud of dust.

A mile later, the Falicon truck came to a security check point. A guard waved it through, directing the driver to a grassy area where a dozen company vehicles were already parked. Beyond this point were hundreds of square kilometers of what used to be a virgin forest.

The men got out, removing their equipment from the back of the truck. When everyone was ready, they trudged through the eerily quiet forest.

Mike, the head engineer, sniffed the air. "God, something smells terrible!"

The team cautiously approached the lake, observing the disaster spread out before them. The water was covered with an iridescent film of oil that was decomposing into a foul, brown sludge along the shoreline, which was littered with a few dead Canadian geese and a loon gasping for air while struggling to flap its oil-covered wings. A bloated beaver carcass bobbed in the lake. Dead walleye, sauger and lake trout floated on the surface. The surrounding vegetation lay rotting in the sun. The cleanup crew, fully protected inside their bio-hazard suits, used rakes to cull the tar balls.

The scientist stared at the mess shaking his head. He tried to contain his anger, but his voice trembled as he said, "I gave my recommendations early on. I told headquarters we had no 'Plan B', but they went ahead anyway." He lost control. "Fuck the animals! Fuck the planet!" He threw his hard hat down. "Do they really expect us to fix the earth!?"

The ground shuddered, alarming the scientist, who shouted, "Did you feel that!?"

Mike answered, "Yeah...strange."

Lightning blazed out of the clear blue sky, striking the water. Thunder boomed as the oil slick ignited, creating

3

a lake of fire. The flames reached the shoreline, following channels of oil runoff, spreading through the forest until one of the fire streams reached an oil reservoir where it exploded, creating a mammoth ball of fire that billowed over the forest. The force of the combustion knocked down the engineers, scientist and cleanup crew. Thick, black smoke descended upon the dazed team members, who struggled to their feet, coughing and choking. The earth violently shook again. Everyone raced out of the man-made hell.

The sound of the oil spill explosion reverberated throughout the Bear Claw First Nation's reservation, which was located a mile from the lake in the middle of the forest where the tribe lived in dilapidated houses that were clustered together like a herd of buffalo protecting their young from the wolves. Crooked stove pipes stuck out of the rooftops with missing shingles. Broken-down cars and rusted-out trucks were parked haphazardly in the weeds. Children, startled by the blast, immediately stopped chasing a ball. Men playing poker and drinking beer under the shade of a tree were stunned into silence as they watched the fireball arch over the trees. Finally, one of the men voiced what the others were thinking, "I knew the oil company would screw up. They always do."

"It's time for a council meeting," stated Tom Running Deer, "It's time for this to end."

Chapter 2

The Magic Seeds

Mahakanta Suresh stood at the edge of his field staring at the withered cotton crop. His farm had been handed down through many generations, providing not only a living, but a good way of life in India's Cotton Belt. He leaned heavily on his hoe, reminiscing of a time long ago when his father had danced with his mother after a bountiful harvest. The entire village had prospered that year, celebrating late into the night with food, spirits and music. His father had stepped away from the festivities and sauntered over to him, holding out a velvety fig he had picked fresh from a banyan branch. Mahakanta plucked the sweet, earthy tasting treat from his father's weathered hand, watching him laugh heartily, drunk from the free-flowing wine.

Mahakanta savored his childhood memory before it faded, leaving him to face the devastation in front of him. He could have survived the misfortune of one bad season, but alas, last year's crop had also failed. Now there was no money left to buy new seeds. He would lose his farm and house to the moneylenders who had extended him credit.

He could no longer face his wife and three children, who silently ate their dinner each night while hopelessness filled the air. His family once had a future, but without property, they would be burdened with a husband and father who couldn't support or provide for them. They would become the lowest of the low.

A sacred cow wandered past him. The bells on its collar clinked as it headed toward his neighbor's field, which was filled with thriving cotton grown from traditional seeds. Mahakanta remembered the purveyor arriving at his doorstep two years earlier, catching him as he returned home after a hard day's work. The salesman opened his satchel, showing Mahakanta charts and photos of other customers' cotton fields that yielded 10 times the average using his new magic seeds. In addition, he touted that the magic seeds resisted pests, eliminating the need to purchase expensive pesticides. The purveyor promised the magic seeds would make Mahakanta a very wealthy man, but what the salesman did not tell him was that these seeds were not drought tolerant like the traditional ones that had been used for generations in India. And the man did not share the fact that the seeds were genetically structured to self-destruct, ensuring that Mahakanta would have to buy new seeds the following year.

So with hope for a better future, Mahakanta naively bought and planted the magic seeds, watching the green shoots emerge in the spring. However, it was not long before the plants withered in the scorching sun and succumbed to the hungry bollworms.

How Mahakanta wished he had switched back to the traditional seeds after the first failed crop, but the purveyor assured him that the dismal harvest was caused by the drought, not the magic seeds, and the next bountiful crop would more than make up for his losses. Mahakanta's misplaced trust had been a deadly mistake. His only comfort was that he wasn't the only one who had fallen under the spell of the magic seeds. Dozens of other farmers in his village had done the same thing.

Knowing he could not survive this second disaster, Mahakanta unscrewed the cap on a pesticide bottle, took one last look at the land of his ancestors, then gulped the toxic fluid. The acid scorched his throat as he swallowed, and the noxious fumes made him gag and cough violently. He thought it was a fitting punishment for his failure, expecting to be dead before his family came back from working in the fields.

Instead, his son found him writhing on the ground in agonizing pain. His wife ran over screaming for help. A neighbor who had found Mahakanta not long after he drank the pesticide explained what had happened. There was nothing anyone could do—the poison always took its victim.

The wife held Mahakanta's head in her lap and wailed, tears streaking down her cheeks, "I told you the money wasn't important! Why didn't you listen!?"

Mahakanta did not respond. The pain made him oblivious to his surroundings. He convulsed violently, spewing red-speckled vomit all over the front of his shirt.

His wife continued to sob, rocking back and forth in utter grief.

Mahakanta was overcome with pain. Everything went dark. He felt his body become weightless. A blue mist appeared, forming into shapes that turned into human forms. He recognized a neighbor who had committed suicide a few weeks earlier. Countless numbers of spirits came forward, one after another, each a victim of crop failure caused by the magic seeds. Before Mahakanta could ask why they came, they escorted him away.

CHAPTER 3

The Organic Farm

On a sunny August morning, the Thompson family was busy harvesting their organic crops. Marilyn and her husband, Larry, had retired early from their stressful jobs in New York City and bought this quaint farm in Pennsylvania to get back to nature, pouring half of their life savings into the venture.

Marilyn rested while wiping the sweat from her face with a handkerchief. She stuffed it back in her pocket while looking out over the rolling hills, admiring the fertile farm beds filled with tomatoes, radishes, green beans and squash. All of this organic produce would be sold at a local farmers' market. Bees buzzed and butterflies floated over the late blooms. She watched her 17-year-old son, Zachary, select ripe tomatoes, setting them in a wagon. He had grown a few inches taller than his father, but he had her sandy-blond hair and fine features.

Car tires scrunched over the crushed limestone driveway, coming to a stop. Dust floated around the tires. An older couple got out of the vehicle, standing side by side looking solemn.

Marilyn, Larry and Zachary waved at their neighbors, Burt and Nancy Wheeler, who returned the greeting, but remained where they stood. Something was wrong.

Larry said to his wife, "This can't be good...looks like their best milk cow died."

Marilyn replied, "Shhh...this might be serious. Come on."

The Thompsons walked out of the field, passing the red barn that housed the milk cow. The chickens scratching in the yard scurried away clucking.

The neighbors met them halfway.

Larry shook the man's hand. "Good morning."

Burt said, "Morning. Sorry we didn't call first, but we've got something important to tell you."

"Okay..."

"This would be better sitting down."

The Thompson family suddenly felt a sense of dread.

Larry responded, "Sure, this way." He led his neighbors through the back door of the centennial farmhouse. They entered the kitchen, taking their seats at the long plank table. Marilyn asked the neighbors if they would like something to drink, but they shook their heads.

Burt started the conversation, "We've been having problems with our cows, one died, and a few had stillborn calves. We heard other farmers had the same thing, so we tested our well and lake. And well..." Bert found it difficult to say the words, "The results showed toxic chemicals and methane gas." The dairy farmer became visibly upset, his voice wavering as he said, "We've lived here for four generations and never had a problem with our water before they started fracking."

"How can that be?" Marilyn asked, "They aren't even drilling close to us!"

"Yeah...well," answered Burt, "we did some research and found out that Pennsylvania allows horizontal drilling, so a rig can be a mile or more away, but drill right under your house without your permission, if you don't own the mineral rights." He rubbed his forehead, noticeably stressed. "We own ours, and told them, 'Thanks, but no thanks.' We didn't want their money. The farm's enough for us. But obviously someone near us either took the money or didn't own the rights."

"But where'd the chemicals come from?" Larry asked.

"The fracking water. They pump millions of gallons of water, laced with chemicals, so they can extract more gas out of the shoal. Then they have the nerve to tell us it's all suctioned up, but common sense tells 'ya it can't be, not all of it. And if they hit an underground stream or aquifer, the contaminated water can flow for miles."

His wife confided, "We plan on moving our cows to my cousin's place in Dauphin County. We can't in good conscience sell the milk. But what'll we do? Farming's all we know." She bit her bottom lip, trying not to cry.

Burt changed the subject, delicately asking the Thompsons, "Have you tested your water? I only ask because our land butts up to yours."

The awareness that the organic farm might be ruined settled over Marilyn like a dark fog. *How can we claim the produce is organic if there are chemicals in the water? How can we sell it at all?* She contemplated these troubling questions before quietly saying, "We didn't give in. We refused to let them test our land and still..." she trailed off.

Zachary put his arm around his mother to comfort her.

11

CHAPTER 4

The Weeping Tree

With teary eyes, Zachary aimlessly followed the tractor trail that ran along the edge of the farm field until he noticed a deer path leading into the woods. Anxious for a distraction, he tracked the meandering trail over fallen trees and under thorny bushes, eventually coming to a glorious tree that stood in a clearing. He grabbed the lowest limb, climbing up, finding a sturdy branch where he sat gazing through the forest, admiring the surrounding fields that flowed one into another. His heart ached at the thought of losing the farm. *Why, God? Why are these jerks allowed to ruin it all?*

A strange blue haze swirled across the sky, its misty fingers slowly descending, reaching for the young man. A gust of wind burst through the haze, dispersing it, before blowing into the forest, whistling through the branches and rustling the leaves. The sound mesmerized Zachary, who unexpectedly connected to the tree's consciousness, feeling her agony as the tainted groundwater burned her roots. He heard her weep, "I'm dying. I'm dying."

Meanwhile, not too far away, Billy White Smoke sat

in a trance on a rocky cliff. He wore a black, brimmed hat decorated with turquoise and silver conchos pulled low over his face. A gray-tinged braid fell down his brawny back. An old, trusty Indian motorcycle rested at the bottom of the hill waiting for him to return.

Billy heard a barely audible call for help that sounded like a woman's voice. He responded, "Where are you? How can I help?" A multitude of voices answered all at once, desperate to capture his attention. Overwhelmed, he shouted, "Silence!" and instantly it was quiet. "Let me hear you," Billy said to the woman. She once again cried, "I'm dying. I'm dying." His link to the voice strengthened, and as it did, a vision of the tree appeared. Billy's spirit reached out to comfort her. "It's all right. Nothing dies, we only transform." Then he noticed Zachary sitting in her branches. Curious, Billy connected to the energy between the young man and the tree, discovering that Zachary was upset about the farmland being ruined. Billy's spirit tried to console him, but his energetic presence alarmed the young man, who sensed someone near him, but couldn't see anyone.

Zachary called out, "Who's there!?"

Billy's presence became stronger and his face materialized in front of Zachary, who froze in fear until he saw the man take off his hat, bowing his head to pray, "Great Spirit, hear our call. Hear the voice of your trees. Hear the voice of your creatures. Please help me to know what to do, where to go and what to say." When Billy opened his eyes, he saw Zachary staring directly at him.

"Please help us!" he pleaded.

Billy infused his thoughts into the young man's mind. *Meet me at the Tipsy Buffalo Pub tomorrow night at seven. Don't be late!* Then his ghost-like presence dissolved into thin air.

13

CHAPTER 5

Bribing Señor Petrola

Señor Petrola was the newly appointed Minister of Culture for the Republic of Peru. His office was located in the administration building in Lima's old downtown, taking advantage of the low-rent space. The minister fanned his face in the hot, dimly lit room while looking out the window at the desolate city below. Few tourists traveled to the historic district, instead preferring the restaurants, galleries and bars that had recently been constructed by foreign investors closer to the beach.

It was not in the budget to retrofit the obsolescent building with central air conditioning, which meant the minister had to rely on the insufficient window units to battle the afternoon sun. He moved the metal fan on his desk from one side to the other, hoping to counteract the heat rising from the first floor. As the fan oscillated, his paperwork sailed into the air, fluttering to the floor. He got up to gather the papers, perspiring even more.

He stacked the papers into neat piles on his desk away from the fan, smiling as he placed a painted rock on each pile, remembering the day Maria, one of his eight children, gave him the handmade birthday gift set. With paint-stained hands, she had set the rocks on the kitchen table for him to admire.

Two men, who appeared to be Americans by the style of their clothes and sweaty, pale faces, entered his office. Señor Petrola greeted them wondering how they got past the receptionist.

One of the men said in Spanish, *"¡Perdón!* Sorry to barge in, Señor Petrola, but there was no one at the front desk. Perhaps the receptionist took a break. No?"

The minister forced a smile. *"Buenas tardes.* What can I do for you?"

"Please excuse our intrusion. My name is Bill Taylor and this is my associate, Larry Reynolds. We're from the Resourcex Corporation."

"Please have a seat," the minister diplomatically offered. The men sat on the worn, wooden chairs. "Would you like something to drink? Bottled water...cola? I can have Isabella bring it in."

Bill replied, "No, thanks. Let me get to the point. We have a wonderful opportunity for this community and possibly you as well." The other man silently nodded in agreement. "All we're asking for is your official endorsement to explore the rainforest. Just to see what's out there."

Señor Petrola cleared his throat knowing his answer would not please them. "The rainforest is home to indigenous people who've lived there thousands of years, and it's protected by international law."

Bill smiled, but his eyes remained cold. "Of course. We don't mean them any harm. Just a little exploration couldn't

15

hurt. And we'll make sure to pay the fees, including those of inconveniencing you, just to hunt and peck for a few weeks. No harm could come of that, now could it?"

"Actually, it could be very dangerous. The tribes will protect their land, even kill for it. It's not a good idea. People could get hurt."

"There are lots of ways to get hurt. You could have a tragic accident on the way home. Nobody can predict these things." The minister's heart rate increased at the not-so-veiled threat. "But we do know our company can't succeed playing by the rules, Señor Petrola. Rules are meant to be broken. Now you're the man who protects the tribes and we'd like your help."

Señor Petrola despised these corrupt bullies and was about to tell them to leave when Bill said, "Since you're a family man, I assume you want what's best for your children. I believe your oldest daughter is fifteen." His associate got up to close the door. Bill waited for him to sit back down. "We can offer you a substantial amount of money for nothing more than letting us see what's in that jungle of yours. If nothing's there, nobody's the wiser."

Visibly tense, Señor Petrola answered, "I don't have the power to allow you to remove natural resources from the rainforest...that involves people with a lot more authority."

"Don't worry. We'll take care of it, should it come to that." Bill pulled out a notepad from his breast pocket to write on. He tore off the top sheet, then slid it face down on the desk. "Take a look. I think you'll like what you see."

Señor Petrola picked up the paper, stunned.

"That's more than you'll make in five years, and it can be yours tomorrow. Think what it'll mean for you and your family...you could create a kids' college fund, a new life for yourself, away from this godforsaken heat and corruption." Bill laughed at his own joke, then stopped, becoming serious again. "The mayor's already on board and won't be happy if you undermine this opportunity. All you have to do is publicly support our exploration. We've prepared statements for you, just in case the media or environmental nuts harass you."

Señor Petrola seethed inside, but he couldn't figure a way out of this predicament. If he said no, his life and family might be in jeopardy and the mayor would make his job hell, probably eliminating any possibility of his appointment being renewed. He felt sorry for the indigenous tribes living in the Amazon rainforest. *They're helpless against the greed and corruption headed their way. But who am I to stop this?* he rationalized. *As long as mankind exists, it'll always be this way.*

"Do we have an agreement?" Bill asked.

The minister solemnly nodded his head.

17

CHAPTER 6

Invading the Rainforest

In a remote part of the Amazon rainforest, indigenous hunters wearing loincloths and necklaces strung with seeds and animal teeth stealthily traversed through the jungle stalking deer, peccaries and monkeys. The men had red and black lines painted across their cheeks and foreheads. The leader, Takwa, wore a colorful feathered headdress. He steadied his blowgun, aiming a lethal dart at a monkey perched in an Aguaje palm tree eating its juicy fruit. The primate felt the hunter's stare and turned toward him, revealing her suckling baby. An iridescent Blue Morpho butterfly fluttered near her face. Takwa lowered his blowgun. The monkey scampered away clutching her young. The hunters would search for more suitable game to feed the tribe.

Standing quietly, Takwa waited for his heart to guide him, but instead he heard a faint rumbling noise in the distance that sounded like a pride of jaguars manically purring. He beckoned the other men, who gathered around him. "There is an intruder. Let us see who it is."

The hunters stepped lightly in the direction of the noise, carefully concealing themselves among the foliage. Noxious fumes drifted through the air. The rumbling grew louder.

Takwa gestured with his hand toward the forest's canopy. He and the men climbed the thick vines hanging from the giant Kapok, Mahogany and Brazil-Nut trees.

High in the towering branches, the hunters saw the intruders—a bulldozer leading three armored SUVs with Resourcex Corporation decals affixed to the sides. The hunters had no reference for what they saw. The vehicles seemed like great beasts clawing and chewing through the dense underbrush, carving out a trail between the ancient trees. The cries of frightened animals and birds echoed through the jungle. A flock of parrots flew away. Screeching monkeys fled. The bulldozer jerked to a stop. Its engine coughed, spewing black exhaust into the air. Behind it, armed guards jumped out of an SUV, ready to protect their precious convoy.

19

Unarmed indigenous workers exited from another vehicle, grabbing rolls of cable from the cargo area, slinging them over their shoulders. The men walked along the newly created trail, running seismic lines that held small dynamite charges. After the workers finished laying the lines, they retreated to the shade.

A man in one of the SUVs pushed a button, detonating the charges, sending clumps of soil into the air.

Takwa had seen enough. He imitated a Macaw parrot. The birdcall grabbed the attention of the other hunters. Next he mimicked the Yellow-rumped Caique. The hunters readied their blowguns. As soon as the third birdcall rang out, poisoned darts sailed silently at the intruders.

A dart struck a guard's neck. He crumpled to the ground.

Two indigenous workers were hit. They collapsed, immobilized by the deadly toxin coursing through their bodies.

A guard fired a warning shot.

The crew rushed toward the vehicles. Once inside, the leader pulled out his satellite phone. As soon as the call connected, he shouted, "The natives are attacking! What should we do!?"

Sitting in a posh office with an incredible view of Houston, Texas, a silver-haired Resourcex executive answered, "Randy, we've discussed this before. You know what to do." He ended the call.

Randy yelled at the guards, "Let's do it!"

One of the guards grabbed a submachine gun hidden under a tarp in the back of the SUV. He jumped out of the vehicle, shooting at a rate of 10 bullets per second toward the treetops. Leaves fell like confetti. Branches splintered, crashing down.

High in the trees, Takwa and the other hunters did not understand how a man could shoot fire. The trees seemed to fall apart before their eyes. A bullet struck one of the hunters. Two more men were shot. All of them fell to the forest floor.

The gunman spat at the ground. "Sons of bitches. I know there's more of 'em!" He renewed his efforts, firing another round. A fourth man dropped, hitting a branch before landing with a thud.

"Good one!" another guard jeered. "That'll teach them!"

The armed guards listened for sounds that might indicate there were more men hiding in the treetops, but all of the animals, birds and hunters had fled. It was silent. The Resourcex contractors waited until they felt it was safe, then investigated their kill.

"Smaller than I expected," a guard mentioned, poking a dead hunter with his gun.

"Yeah, tough little suckers," another one commented.

"Look! Here's a dead monkey. Wonder if the hide's worth anything?"

"Don't know if I'd be caught with that..."

"Yeah. I'd probably get in more trouble for this here monkey skin than these dead Indians." He laughed.

"Stop screwing around," Randy said sternly. "Let's take our men back and return tomorrow. Doubt the natives will give us any more trouble."

During the commotion, Takwa and the other surviving hunter had snuck away, traveling deep into the jungle where their people had lived for thousands of years undisturbed by the outside world.

Survival in the rainforest depended on the tribe's knowledge of dangers lurking in every crevice. Jaguars hid in the trees ready to pounce on passing prey. Anacondas, crocodiles, piranhas, stinging ants, poisonous snakes, frogs and spiders inflicted bodily harm and death in all the corners of the tropical jungle. Occasionally the Nawatia tribe lost a baby or pet to a predator, but, for the most part, they lived harmoniously with the creatures of the rainforest. However, the new danger—the convoy of hollow beasts carrying men who used magic sticks to shoot fire—scared the hunters more than all the others. The indigenous men raced through the forest's dense foliage, skillfully navigating its slippery ground, finally reaching the village where they hurried past the thatch huts, women cooking and children playing, heading toward their spiritual leader, Pahtia, who lived on the outskirts. He would know what to do.

Pahtia sat in his hut receiving a message from the spirits, "Danger is coming! Beware the new beast!" He raised his gray-haired head as the two hunters ran to his doorway, stopping outside, gasping for breath. The shaman opened his eyes. "Come in. What is wrong?"

Takwa entered still breathing heavily, "There are men in the forest...men carrying magic sticks. Sticks that shoot fire! They killed four of us! These men...will come kill us all!"

"Do they have magic eyes as well?" Pahtia asked, irritated by their fumbled hunting expedition. "How did they see you?"

"No eyes are needed...to blindly shoot fire."

"How did they know you were there?" Pahtia inquired further.

"We shot darts...killing three men."

The shaman stared blankly while a vision came to him, showing him what had happened. "We need to talk with the elders. This is a tribal matter," he snapped, "Hurry to tell them. I will follow."

Takwa rushed out of the hut as Pahtia's daughter, Conchita, a young woman with a flower tucked in her flowing black hair, came through the doorway holding a basket filled with fresh herbs. The hunter looked at her with adoring eyes wishing he could stay. She watched him race away, then asked her father, "What is wrong?"

"There is a grave threat coming. I must ask the spirits for guidance. Please join me."

She sat next to her father, placing the basket in front of him. Pahtia gently sifted through the contents. He selected a few leaves, sniffing to confirm their identity, then dropped them into the fire. He closed his eyes, breathing in the smoke, waiting for the visions to come.

A fog rolled across the ground. A black jaguar strolled out of the forest through the haze, prowling toward Pahtia's hut, sneaking through the doorway. The panther silently approached the shaman, coming up behind him, listening to the blood pulsating through his veins. The big cat opened her mouth over his frail neck, then licked him.

"Ooh, Taslia! You sneaky cat!" Pahtia laughed, wiping the saliva from his neck. The jaguar purred, rubbing her head against his. Taslia was Pahtia's totem animal—his protector and guide through the spirit realm. Conchita smiled as she watched the loving interaction between her father and the totem animal.

23

"Taslia, old friend! Today, I need your help more than ever. Can you take me to my spirit guide?" She nodded.

Pahtia stood and straddled the jaguar's strong back. Conchita sat behind her father, wrapping her arms around him. The totem animal strolled out of the hut, journeying through the mist into a realm resembling a mystical rainforest, leading them to a waterfall that flowed into a sparkling lake lined with lush ferns. Pahtia had been here many times before. It was the home of his spirit guide. He called out, "Maka! Please come! We need your help!"

The spirit guide appeared in the shape of a beautiful woman floating over the water. She wore white, fringed animal skins decorated with colorful feathers and beads. Her black hair hung to her knees. She gave him a warm smile. "Greetings!"

Pahtia bowed his head out of respect, then pleaded, "Please help us! Strangers are invading our home. Strangers who possess power greater than ours."

Maka softly replied, "I will help your tribe, but you and the elders must stay with me for three moons."

Pahtia was quiet.

"What is the matter?"

"We do not have time for that! The men and beasts will find us and kill us!"

"Do you doubt me?" she asked.

"I believe you, but the tribe might not."

"You are a very persuasive man, Pahtia. Find a way to convince them."

In the main area near the fire pit, the chief and elders shook their heads in confusion as they listened to the two hunters describe the intruders. The shaman approached with Conchita by his side. Everyone hushed. Pahtia broke the silence, "The hunters speak the truth. I saw it in a vision."

Chief Jebero said, "Tell us your vision."

"There were great beasts with no heads and hollow bodies that carried men through the jungle. The men held sticks that shot fire. Their power is strong, but not as strong as the spirit guide, Maka. She agreed to help us if we stay with her for three moons."

"Three moons!? With intruders coming!?"

"It is much to ask, but if we fight, we will be killed. Who will protect our women and children if the men are dead?" Pahtia asked.

"Is the enemy that strong?"

"These men fight alongside dead, yet moving creatures. How do you fight something that has no soul?

If we fight face to face, we will lose. But there is hope. Maka will use her power...a power greater than any here on Earth. We can either trust her, fight or run away. The choice is yours."

The chief contemplated the shaman's words. It would be dangerous to flee with so many people traveling through the territories of rival tribes. If the other tribes learned they had run from their enemy, it wouldn't be long before they hunted in their territory and attacked them. Only the strong survived in the jungle.

"If the power of Maka fails us, we will lose our home and our lives," Chief Jebero stated. The elders nodded in agreement.

Pahtia gazed at his beloved child and said, "We must do this to survive."

The chief stomped his staff on the ground three times, proclaiming, "So it is." He turned toward Pahtia. "Lead us to the spirit realm. May the spirits bless us!" Then the chief instructed the hunters to gather more men to bring back the bodies of the dead tribesmen.

25

Takwa and the other men slowed their pace as they neared the area where their fellow hunters had been killed. Here it was oddly quiet, except for the squawking vultures that were fighting over the corpses. The men grabbed sticks, which they waved menacingly while shouting to scare away the scavengers. The carnivorous birds took to flight, flapping their broad wings, leaving behind a gruesome sight. The dead men's entrails had been eaten, and their broken arms and legs were twisted in odd positions. Flies swarmed.

The men knelt to pray, then got to work cutting bark from trees. The inside of the bark contained fibers, which they wove into rope. Bamboo was cut down to be used as poles. They tied the bark to the poles, creating impromptu slings for carrying the dead men through the jungle's dense foliage.

As Takwa set the last dead man in a sling, a drop of fresh blood dripped onto the corpse's face. Takwa looked up and saw an unconscious Capuchin monkey slumped in the crotch of a tree—his small, black arms and legs dangling from the branches. A bullet had grazed his white-furred shoulder, and there was a jagged wound across his milky face. A baby monkey cowered under his body, shaking with fear.

Wondering if the adult monkey was alive, the hunter prodded him with a stick. There was no reaction, except for the slightest movement of his head. Takwa looked around for the infant's mother, saddened to see her lying on the ground dead and covered with ants.

The other men patiently waited while Takwa gently lifted the monkeys from the tree, setting them beside one of their fallen comrades. Takwa knew that if the adult monkey was still alive when they returned, the women would tend to his wounds, believing it would please the spirits.

At dusk, the men arrived in the village carrying their solemn load. The women wailed at the sight of the dead hunters, who were laid in the communal hut. There the women began lovingly washing the bodies, arranging trinkets, stones and flowers around them. The unconscious male monkey was placed in a corner with a poultice on his wounds to prevent an infection. The baby monkey was given to a woman, who would breastfeed the little one alongside her own infant.

When the moon appeared, the chief and elders joined Conchita and Pahtia inside their hut, solemnly sitting around the small fire pit. They all closed their eyes. Soon a white mist appeared and their spirits rose out of their bodies, entering the spirit realm where the totem animal, Taslia, waited for them.

The black jaguar's outline shimmered in the moonlight as she guided them through the shadowy rainforest, heading toward the waterfall. Birds screeched and clucked. Monkeys hooted. Insect noises radiated from every direction. The group traveled on, intent on reaching their destination.

When they arrived at the waterfall, Pahtia stood at the edge of the dark lake summoning the spirit guide.

Maka appeared floating over the black water. She lovingly gazed at them, saying, "Greetings!"

Pahtia replied, "Greetings! Thank you for helping us."

"It is my pleasure. For three moons, we will combine our energies to manifest a different destiny. Are you ready?" The Nawatia tribe members nodded. "Let us begin."

The next morning at the Resourcex camp, Randy woke up ready to start the workday, but the smile left his face when he heard the rain hitting his tent. Annoyed, he put on his jacket and boots, stepping outside. He didn't see anyone, except for his right-hand man, Pete, who solemnly greeted him, "Morning, Boss," raising his cup of coffee as rain dripped off his hat.

"Damn it! Does it ever stop raining?" Randy scowled.

"It is a rainforest," Pete pointed out.

"Yeah, as soon as this storm stops, we'll get back to work."

27

"Well...we got a problem. The locals left in the middle of the night and took their dead with 'em."

Randy cursed, "God damn cowards!"

Lightning streaked through the sky, hitting the bulldozer. Sparks flew out of its engine. Randy and Pete instinctively crouched down. The other crewmen rushed out of their tents to see what had happened.

Still holding his coffee mug, Pete looked at the blackened bulldozer. "Well, looks like we got another problem."

Thunder clapped and the rain began coming down in buckets. The men hurried inside their tents. A soaked Randy punched a number on his satellite phone, planning to inform his boss of the weather delays, but the reception failed, so he decided to catch up on his paperwork while he waited for the rain to stop.

28

However, the rain didn't stop. By nightfall, the saturated ground caused the tents to collapse, forcing the men to seek refuge in the SUVs, making them a surly bunch.

When the crew awoke the next morning, the rainstorm had worsened into a torrential downpour. They sat in the SUVs unable to see out the steamy windows. After hours of staring at each other, everyone had an extreme case of cabin fever. "I can't take anymore!" Randy bellowed, "The next guy who farts is a dead man!" The men snickered.

A groan erupted from beneath the vehicle. "Shhh! What's that sound?" Pete asked. The groan came again. He tried to open his door, but it wouldn't budge. He asked Randy to turn on the power, so he could roll down the window. Pete stuck his head out. Rain pelted his face. He could barely see a few inches, much less the ground. To get a better look, he climbed out the window. His legs quickly submerged into the soupy soil. "Oh, my God! We're sinking!" he shouted, scrambling to get back inside the SUV, but he was stuck. "Help me!"

Randy pulled on Pete's arms, slowly easing him out of the quicksand. A sucking sound erupted as the earth released its hold on him.

Covered with mud and soaking wet, Pete sighed with relief as he closed the window until he heard another groan and felt the SUV shudder.

"We're screwed!" one of the men cried out. "We're sinking with no way out!"

"Let's get on the roof and pray the rain stops before... well...you know," Randy suggested. "Whatever you do, don't fall!"

Climbing out the window, each man scaled the slippery vehicle, blindly grabbing the luggage rack, pulling himself onto the rooftop. There they sat soaked, hoping for the best.

In the morning, the sun's hot rays shone through the clear skies, baking the topsoil of the campsite that was void of any signs of life, tents, vehicles or the bulldozer. It didn't take long for the porous sand to drain away the excess water, creating a crusty surface that concealed what lay below.

Pahtia, Conchita and the elders returned from the spirit realm. Chief Jebero spoke first, "Pahtia, you were right. The spirit's power is great! May we live in peace again!"

Pahtia praised Maka for her help, but voiced a concern to the chief, "I fear more intruders will come."

The chief thought this over. "Let us put warriors near the trail. If outsiders come, our men will warn us." The elders seemed satisfied with this solution, however, Pahtia remained worried, but after three days with no food, he and everyone else were famished.

When they returned home, the women told them that the two monkeys had survived, then prepared a bountiful, celebratory breakfast of fruit, berries and smoked meats, served with a fermented beverage. The tribe feasted. For now, they were safe.

CHAPTER 7

The Tipsy Buffalo Pub

Zachary nervously drove his parents' pickup, slowing down as he entered the city limits. A robotic voice from his phone instructed, "Turn right onto Meadow Street." Zachary followed the directions wondering why he was entering a residential neighborhood. "Turn left onto Industrial Drive." The street came to a "T" at the railroad tracks. He turned left. Within a few blocks, the houses became sparse as the district gave way to a lumberyard. "You have reached your destination." The Tipsy Buffalo Pub was discretely tucked between two commercial buildings.

Zachary swallowed hard looking at the shabby building surrounded by heavy-duty work trucks and hog motorcycles. He pulled into the gravel parking lot, found a parking spot and turned off the engine. He took a deep breath before getting out, then hesitantly walked toward the entrance trying to decide if he had the guts to enter.

A sign over the doorway read, "If you don't know if you belong here, you don't." He disregarded it, as well as the faded plastic sign nailed to the door that stated, "You must be 21 to enter," and went inside.

He waited for his eyes to adjust to the dark, smoky room, trying to appear confident, which was difficult with a half dozen, tough-looking men staring at him. Zachary recognized the man from his vision sitting at the bar, holding a beer. The man turned toward him, tipping his black hat. Zachary took a seat next to him.

"What'll you have, kid?" the man asked.

"A Coke," Zachary answered, trying to ignore the snickers from the other men.

The bartender poured the soft drink while the man in the black hat introduced himself, "Name's Billy White Smoke." He held out his hand.

Zachary shook it. "I'm Zachary Thompson. Nice to meet you."

Billy began the conversation. "It seems the world's gone crazy. Never been a sane place, but now they're not content to just kill people. Now they're killing everything in sight...the trees, water, air. Jesus help us. It's gotta end."

"Jesus?" asked Zachary, "I thought you guys believed in the Great Spirit."

Billy smiled, causing the dangerous look on his face to disappear. "Jesus, the buffalo, the trees, our ancestors... all are teachers. Wisdom is wisdom."

Zachary glanced around the bar. "Why'd you choose this place?"

"It's one of the few places the government spooks won't enter."

Zachary suddenly became concerned that Billy wasn't mentally stable.

32

Billy noticed the expression on the young man's face. "Think it's a conspiracy theory? Once you're labeled a rebel—someone protesting corporate greed and abuse of power—you'll notice the dark, unmarked cars following you." He lit a cigarette. The smoke calmed him. "Freedom is an illusion. Try walking along the road with long hair and it won't be long before a sheriff pulls up asking questions." The smoke curled around his face. "Try living your life in touch with nature. The government's made it illegal to use our sacred plants. They're afraid we'll use them and remember how powerful we are. Meanwhile, they destroy the earth for profit and offer us chemicals to heal ourselves. Enough is enough. It's time to take back our land, our way of life. The white man has proven he can't handle the responsibility." Billy looked at Zachary's light complexion. "No offense."

Zachary fidgeted with the straw in his drink unsure of what to do or say.

"Look, I want to help you and your family, and maybe, just maybe, there's still time, but even if your land is doomed, there are others that can be saved. That's my mission—to help what's left and stop this insane destruction."

Zachary's heart ached over the possible loss of his family's beloved farm where he had hoped to work all the days of his life.

"You've gotta admit, you suddenly got a lot of time on your hands," Billy commented, snubbing out his cigarette.

The words stung Zachary, who thought, *No shit, dumbshit.*

Billy drank the last of his beer, setting the glass down. "Kid, if we're going to work together, you've got to watch your language."

CHAPTER 8

Visiting the Tree

It was a sunny, crisp morning when Billy knocked on Zachary's front door.

Marilyn answered, "Yes? Can I help you?"

"Morning, ma'am. I'm here to see Zachary. Name's Billy White Smoke."

She looked at the man's long, braided hair and black hat wondering how he knew her son. "Just a moment."

She shut the door, then went upstairs to Zachary's room. His door was ajar, so she peeked inside expecting him to be asleep, but instead she found him sitting by the window gazing down at the fields of the family's farm. "Zach, there's a man here to see you. Says his name's Billy—"

"Yep!" he interrupted, briskly walking past her and down the stairs before she could ask questions.

Zachary stepped outside.

Billy was kneeling on the porch petting the dogs. He stood up, smiling. "Good morning! Let's go honor the tree." He held up his fringed, deerskin medicine bag.

The two men strolled in the field alongside the woods. The dogs tagged along until they caught a whiff of an enticing scent, wagging their tails as they ran in a different direction.

Zachary kept searching the edge of the trees for the deer path that would lead them to the weeping tree. When he finally found it, he motioned for Billy to follow him.

Trekking through the forest, Zachary kept a close eye on the obscure trail that often melded into the underbrush. Billy broke the young man's concentration by tapping him on the shoulder, pointing to a herd of deer grazing in a patch of sunlight. The men enjoyed the transcendent moment until a doe raised her head, cautiously looking around with her big, brown eyes, sniffing the air. Suddenly her tail flipped up, exposing the white underside, signaling danger. She bounded away. The rest of the herd followed, leaping over bushes and dashing around trees, disappearing from view.

"Wow! That was amazing!" Zachary exclaimed.

Billy nodded.

They continued walking through the woods. When the path came to the tree, Billy opened his medicine bag, taking out a pinch of tobacco that he sprinkled at the base of the trunk while invoking its spirit, then he listened. After a moment, he said, "She's agreed to let us sit in her branches."

"You asked a tree for permission!?"

Ignoring the question, Billy climbed the tree, sitting on a branch overlooking the hills below, then closed his eyes. Zachary followed his lead, finding a strong limb.

Billy unexpectedly sang out loud, "*Ne, we, can, e, tepa, we, sphe, ma, mi, too...*" He had become a conduit for the

35

ancestors who used his mouth to sing the old language. Billy didn't understand the words, but he understood the meaning as he lifted his voice, "The Great Spirit is a friend of the people. Let us call on our brothers to remember we are one...the land, the water, the air, the four-legged, those that swim, those that soar. The Great Spirit loves us all."

The heartfelt song mesmerized Zachary. As he listened, he felt part of an ancient journey begun long ago and saw his destiny unfolding before him, filling him with both fear and awe. *I hope I have the courage to fulfill my purpose,* he thought.

Billy opened his eyes, smiled ever so slightly, gently saying, "The Great Spirit never asks for more than we can give."

36

After spending the morning meditating in the tree, Billy began telling Zachary about his native heritage. "Life on this land was different before the white man came. We only took what we needed. There was no poverty like you see on the reservations today. We shared from our abundance. We hunted together. We ate together. We sat around the fire at night and told stories that explained how we came to be and how to live as one with nature. When an animal was killed, we thanked it for giving its life...so that we may live."

Zachary asked, "In the vision...when I first saw you... you were on a cliff. What were you doing?"

"I was journeying to the spirit realm. There I commune with spirits of the living, the divine and my ancestors. My spirit wanders among them...learning, listening, asking questions. Sometimes, I go just to remember that I am one with the universe."

"Oh," Zachary responded.

"Would you like to learn?"

"Really!? But I'm white!"

Billy laughed. "Everyone can do it. Although, there are some who have a special gift. Their visions are so strong... they can heal. That's powerful medicine."

37

CHAPTER 9

The Miko

In the misty foothills of the Ōu Mountains stood an ancient Japanese temple surrounded by a meditation garden filled with bonsai and plum trees, lavender and cultivated roses. Wisteria vines clung to the walls and cherry trees draped over the moss-covered stone steps that led to an exquisitely crafted entrance decorated with ornate, yet faded, carvings.

High on the third floor, Haruto gazed out of an open window while basking in the sunlight. She wore a white silk blouse and scarlet flowing trousers with a white sash tied around her waist. Straight, black hair cascaded down her back. Black liner adorned her eyes that had a flourish of red powder on the outer corners. Like her mother, grandmother and great-grandmother, Haruto was a Miko, a tradition dating back thousands of years to when female shamans mingled with the ruling class, acting as healers, mediums and ritual dancers. Over time, the women had been diminished to the role of assistants under the male shamans, which was unacceptable to some of the Miko, such as the women who lived in this temple.

Smoke from Haruto's slender pipe danced around her face, drifting outside as she surveyed the city of Fukushima in the basin below. The hustle and bustle of the metropolis was tempered by the surrounding majestic mountains etched with rivers flowing into the emerald sea tugging at its shoreline.

In the distance, she saw the nuclear power plant that had been damaged years earlier. A record-breaking earthquake had erupted deep in the Pacific Ocean, demolishing houses, structures and roads, and knocking down the power lines, but fortunately, the nuclear plant crew had been able to start the backup generators, avoiding a meltdown. Everything was under control until the tsunami hit, twice. The massive waves killed 20,000 people and flooded the plant, damaging the generators. The lack of electricity caused the reactors to overheat, then explode. The melted cores leaked radiation throughout the facility, making it nearly impossible for anyone to remedy the situation. Fixing it had become a suicide mission. A few brave souls raced in and out, trying to open vents and flip switches, resembling mice retrieving pieces of cheese while a hungry cat lurked in the room. Over time, the situation grew worse. The outside containment areas deteriorated, allowing radioactive water to leak into the sea. The Japanese government had refused offers of international assistance to remedy the disaster, and suffered ever since. Now the sea surrounding the nuclear plant boiled like an oversized cauldron brewing poison.

Tears came to Haruto's eyes. She turned away, moving across her sparse room to a table that held an ancient teapot, tea tin and porcelain cup. She poured hot water into the cup, then dropped in tea leaves, watching them sink to the bottom. Green swirls rose from the leaves, conjuring a replica of the city below. The scene within her cup whisked past rows of houses and the shopping district to where the nuclear plant stood. Outside the facilities, the workers wore white protective suits as they scampered around the leaky containment bins. Their busyness kept them from feeling helpless.

Haruto felt the loving presence of the Spirit surrounding her with divine energy. She heard It whisper, "You are loved, as we love all things. What you see before you is the fear within you, reflected outward."

She winced at the blunt message. "Would you rather have all of us killed by radiation? I must defend the earth!"

"To defend is to believe you are mortal. Only mortals would believe anything has power over them."

"I live in a physical world dealing with harsh realities and the consequences of foolish decisions! I don't want to hurt anyone. I just want this madness to stop!" There was no response. The Voice seemed to have vanished. Haruto immediately regretted her anger.

The Miko walked out of the temple, down the exterior stone steps, following an ancient path that lead to the garden. She came to her favorite spot and stood in the center of the roses. Their gentle fragrance was carried by a breeze that caressed her face. She clasped her hands and bowed her head for a moment, then methodically began moving her arms and legs, as if following an inner guidance. The gestures quickened into martial arts—jumping, kicking and chopping. As the energy intensified, her motions took on the appearance of floating midair, transcending the boundaries of physics. She ran up the garden wall, reaching the top, breathing in the mountain air. She felt alive in the moment, the earth's heartbeat resonating beneath her feet. She viewed the picturesque countryside, feeling at peace until she caught a glimpse of the nuclear plant in the distance. The steam from the boiling sea taunted her, causing her peace to sink like a rock. Her mind screamed, *I must do something!* She expertly jumped off the wall, hurrying through the garden, returning to the temple. A wooden lion-dog head, which protected the grounds from evil spirits, was perched on the corner of the roofline, watching her pass below with its glowing blue eyes.

She rushed up three flights of stone stairs, entering her room where she sat on a mat and beckoned the spirits, "I humbly request your guidance." A vision appeared. Haruto saw herself walking through a fog, passing barren trees while wearing a scarlet cape.

A fire-breathing dragon slithered from the mist. His body was covered with iridescent green scales. On his head were horns that curved over his furry mane. He had multiple rows of razor-sharp teeth and topaz eyes that stared at her while his forked tongue flicked in and out. Haruto contained her fear. "Who dares approach the great deities?" he hissed. His tongue flicked again.

"It is I, Haruto," she answered, holding her head high.

"Who are you to enter?" the dragon challenged.

"Is not everyone worthy?"

A puff of smoke wafted from the dragon's nose as he moved his head from side to side sizing her up. "We'll see what the council says," he snapped, curving his long body to guide the way.

Haruto followed the dragon as he lumbered through the fog swishing his long, spiny tail. An iron gate appeared. Its ornate doors swung open. They proceeded through

41

the gateway. The fog gave way to a forest.

The dragon led Haruto to a clearing where five spirits sat on logs around a fire, announcing, "Haruto has requested to meet you."

Three samurai soldiers stood to bow, holding their helmets by their sides. Each was fitted with a different color of armor—one green, one red and one black—with a long, sheathed sword tucked inside the waistband.

A crone with wild gray hair remained seated, cackling with delight at Haruto's presence. She wore a plain, black dress.

A young priestess in a graceful cream-colored gown approached Haruto, greeting her with a soft voice, "I am glad you came. Please sit with us."

Everyone sat by the fire, except for the dragon. He lay outside the group with his tail curled around his body, promptly falling asleep.

The priestess implored, "Tell us why you've come."

Haruto explained, "Where I live there is a nuclear power plant spilling radioactive waste. I would like your help fixing it."

The priestess picked up a delicate, white porcelain smoking pipe with cherry blossoms painted on its bowl. She plucked a twig from the fire and lit the aromatic tobacco. After a few puffs, she passed it to Haruto, who smoked it, then passed it to the samurai sitting next to her. As the pipe made its rounds, the crone spoke in a hoarse voice, "I believe you received an answer earlier today, one which you ignored."

"You mean when I was told the disaster was a reflection of my mind?" Haruto asked.

The crone chortled, "You do remember!"

Slightly offended, Haruto appealed to the samurai soldiers, "You must understand the need to fight! You made warfare a sacred calling."

The samurai in black armor answered, "In a sense, everything is spiritual. However, attack is always against yourself. Oft times, we must fight a battle, if only to learn to lay down our arms."

The red-armored samurai piped in, "When you understand that fighting's sole purpose is to preserve your own illusions, you will stop fighting."

"What's the point?" Haruto asked, exasperated.

"There is no point, except to learn there is no point," the samurai in green offered.

"Well, I disagree," Haruto said.

"We agree with your right to disagree," they said in unison. Haruto felt mocked.

43

From out of nowhere, a blue door appeared with a thud, resting on the forest floor. Haruto studied it, then asked, "Where does that lead?"

"A place we will not go," answered the priestess.

"Will something bad happen there?"

"That depends on you."

The door swung open, releasing a blue mist that rolled along the ground beckoning Haruto. She walked to the door, glancing back at the council. No one paid any attention to her, except for the dragon who drowsly peered at her as she stepped through the opening, disappearing into the mist. The dragon roused to follow her, slithering past the door before it swung shut, barely missing the tip of his tail.

CHAPTER 10

Bear Claw Council Meeting

An hour after the oil spill explosion, the Bear Claw First Nation elders and leaders began arriving in the community center that had been built in the 1980s. Its walls were lined with outdated wood paneling. Folding chairs were scattered about the dimly lit room. Grandmother Hausis hobbled across the threshold wearing a plain cotton dress. Her salt-and-pepper braids were pinned to the back of her head. Chief Keme walked in wearing his favorite white, buttoned shirt with feathers embroidered on each shoulder. Some of the tribe members debated his ability to lead the tribe fairly, arguing he was too connected to outside leaders and businessmen, but his defenders claimed he had a heart of gold. The remaining elders and council members entered. A few of them had embellished their wardrobes with turquoise and silver jewelry. Tom Running Deer wore a t-shirt that read, "If You're Not Indigenous, You're Illegal!"

Altogether there were six elders, 12 council members and the chief who announced, "Let's get started!" Everyone quieted down and took a seat. Chief Keme began the meeting. "Thank you for coming. As you know, we're here to discuss the oil spill at Bear Claw Lake. It's been over a year, and, as the recent explosion proves, it's still out of control." The chief's statement stirred up deep-rooted anger. Nearly everyone grumbled under his or her breath.

Sixty years earlier, the tribe had leased 10,000 square kilometers of their land to the Canadian government for a weapons range during the Cold War, but when the lease expired 20 years later, the government refused to budge. A lengthy legal battle ensued that resulted in the tribe being compensated with millions of dollars, but the government gained legal ownership. Soon after, oil companies occupied the military base. Now the tribe was left to deal with army trainees shooting bombs over their old burial ground while the oil companies decimated the land. Every time a military plane flew overhead, it was a grim reminder that the tribe had been swindled out of their hunting grounds.

"We want our land back!" shouted a councilman.

Councilwoman Cecile Two Feathers accusingly said to the chief, "I heard rumors you're trying to sell more of our land. It's not for sale!"

A shouting match began, growing louder and more heated as it went along. Grandma Hausis and the other elders listened quietly until one of them began singing in their native tongue. One by one, each elder joined in and the volume increased. The younger council members became ashamed when they saw the old ones gently rising above the conflict. The arguing died out.

Chief Keme respectfully waited until the elders finished singing, then said, "We need the guidance of our elders. We are fighting among ourselves...selfishly. We must remember that we're here to offer wisdom to make better decisions as a tribe."

"Why don't we spell out the problems?" a councilman suggested. "Write them down. Perhaps it will help us to see clearly what needs to be done."

Cecile got up, walking to the board. She wrote, "Oil spill."

"Oil companies!" someone shouted. It was added to the board.

"Military base on our territory!"

"Land stolen by the government!"

"We never should have bargained with our land," Tom solemnly stated.

Everyone stared at the board. The problems seemed insurmountable.

Grandma Hausis finally broke the silence. "It is time to ask the Great Spirit for guidance."

Chief Keme nodded in agreement. "Let's reconvene tomorrow afternoon at the old ceremonial place. We'll ask for a vision."

The next day, the Bear Claw elders and council members headed toward the sacred gathering ground wearing ceremonial clothing adorned with beads, fringe and feathers. Although trees camouflaged the location, it was just a short walk from the community center. Even Grandma Hausis managed to plod along the winding path.

Everyone sat on the logs surrounding the fire pit that was filled with ashes, except for Chief Keme who stood, saying, "We have important decisions to make regarding

46

what's best for the tribe and land. Divine guidance is key to making the best decisions, so I'll be using peyote during our vision quest. You are free to join me." The chief was referring to the "buttons" of the peyote cactus, which had been ritually consumed by the North American indigenous people for over 5,000 years. The sacred plant helped them to more vividly experience the spirit realm where they asked spirit guides for guidance and healing.

To start the ceremony, the chief said a prayer, "Plant Spirit, we call on you to help us understand the ways of this world. Please offer us your wisdom and visions. Help us to break through our selfish minds and remember our divine selves." He nodded at Cecile, who pulled out a glass jar filled with soft nougats of the chewy cactus. She took a few before giving it to Tom. He did the same, passing it to Grandma Hausis who handed it to the person sitting next to her and so on until each member held the buttons in their hands. The chief put the peyote buttons in his mouth. Everyone followed his example, then sat quietly waiting for the effects to begin.

Clouds began rolling through the trees, drifting through the clearing. Sounds from the forest intensified. The people heard spiders building their webs, butterflies flapping their wings and caterpillars munching on leaves. The volume escalated, consuming the council members as the noises combined into one harmonious song that reverberated like a choir of angels, singing higher and higher, reaching a pinnacle note whose vibration was on the verge of shattering the gate to heaven. Suddenly the song ceased, mentally letting them free fall.

"I'm gonna be sick," Cecile uttered. She stumbled a few feet away to throw up, immediately feeling better. When

47

she lifted her head, everything was radiating brilliant colors.

Tom saw the colors as well, exclaiming, "It's all so beautiful!" He tried to touch the glowing particles swirling near his face, but couldn't tell where his hand ended and the universal palette began.

Several members chanted, inviting the ancestors to join them. Chief Keme danced around the fire pit to a phantom drumbeat. The others joyfully crouched like wild animals or flapped their arms like birds, shapeshifting from one consciousness to another, losing themselves in the Oneness.

In the midst of this, vibrant particles swirled together, becoming denser, until they resembled the shape of a stag. The energy strengthened, causing the buck to appear lifelike with gentle eyes and a massive set of antlers that he proudly displayed. His arrival captured the attention of the group.

The stag totem animal proclaimed, "You have asked for an answer, but the answer is not out there, it's within you."

"We didn't destroy our land. They did!" Tom cried out.

The stag patiently responded, "Your medicine men have repeatedly told you, 'Life is a dream.' You must decide whether you are the dream or the dreamer."

Tom became angry. He interpreted two meanings from the stag's message and felt both were offensive, however, out of respect, he kept his thoughts to himself, but the stag knew.

Thud! A blue door dropped from the sky, landing on the forest floor. Everyone stared at it.

Cecile was the first to ask, "Where does that lead?"

48

The stag answered, "To a different realm with a different answer."

Tom replied, "Well, I'm ready for some real answers to our problems. We've sat idle for too long. It's time to act!"

The door unlatched, slowly swinging open. All of the members stared at the blue mist flowing out of the doorway.

Tom stepped closer to the door, but was hesitant to go alone. He turned toward the others and said, "What are you waiting for?" The others stood still, undecided. "If you could solve this problem, wouldn't you?" he prodded, trying to build support. He glanced at the black void past the doorway. "It's part of the spirit realm. How bad could it be?"

One of the councilmen became convinced, shouting, "Let's take back our land!" as he marched toward the door.

Chief Keme took the lead. The others followed him, except for Grandma Hausis who remained sitting.

"Are you going?" the stag asked her.

"I'm too old to fight," she replied matter-of-factly.

The stag nodded, then picked up his hooves, moving through the mist, following the tribe members beyond the blue door.

CHAPTER 11

Journey to the Spirit Realm

The sky was clear and the morning temperature still mild as Zachary drove on the dirt road carved out of a forest. A white, rusted mailbox with hand-painted numbers came into view. He slowed down, pulling into the makeshift driveway that meandered through the trees, coming to a silver bullet trailer set on a small plot of land. An old, well-kept motorcycle and battered pickup truck were stationed out front. Zachary parked behind them. He walked across the yard, viewing the well-tended garden and fire pit, then knocked on the shiny door, prompting a dog to bark inside.

A voice behind him shouted, "Hey!"

Zachary spun around. Billy stood there grinning. The young man let out a deep sigh of relief. "God, you scared me! How'd you sneak up on me like that!?"

"Old Indian trick!" Billy chuckled. "Have any trouble finding the place?"

"No, just further out than I expected."

"Well, glad you made it. Still interested in learning to journey?"

"Yep!"

"Okay, just give me a sec' and we'll head out." Billy went into his trailer. A minute later, he came out carrying a buffalo drum that he strapped over his shoulder. "Let's go!"

The two men ambled through the woods until they found a dry, sturdy log to sit on. Billy rested the drum on his knee, then paused, silently beckoning the ancestors, asking them to bless the lesson. When he felt loving energy enter his heart, he knew the spirits approved of him sharing the sacred wisdom.

Billy began by saying, "First, let me explain the basics of journeying. The way I was taught, you start by calling for your totem animal, who'll act as your guide through the spirit realm."

Zachary interrupted, "What's my body do when I'm in the spirit realm?"

"Same thing it does when you're sleeping...not much."

"Is it possible I won't come back?"

"Anything's possible, but it's not likely. Although, I've heard stories of great shamans who went up mountains and never returned...no one ever found their bodies either." Zachary's eyes grew big. Billy slapped him on the back and laughed. "You worry too much, kid!"

Zachary felt like a rookie.

"When you're ready, I'll guide you through the process. Okay?"

"Okay, I'm ready."

Billy pounded the drum with an elk skin beater. The rhythmic beat hypnotized Zachary, who sat with his eyes closed. Billy spoke with deep reverence, "Try to

51

imagine what I'm saying. Clouds are appearing...let them surround you. Let the mist engulf you. Lose yourself in the loving energy. Now walk forward, trusting you will find firm footing with each step. Walk until the mist fades away, showing you the land of your dreams spread out before you. Explore the surroundings. Here you'll find your totem animal, who has waited a long time to meet you. Your totem animal can be a reptile, insect, fish, mammal, bird or mystical creature. Look around...see what appears. I'll be quiet now."

Billy closed his eyes, losing himself in the drumbeat while Zachary wandered through the mist in the spirit realm, which soon faded away to reveal a magical forest filled with rabbits nibbling on vegetation, butterflies fluttering and birds singing. Billy's voice echoed, "Explore your surroundings...find your totem animal who has waited a long time to meet you."

Zachary enjoyed the scenery as he walked through the ancient forest, coming to a giant oak tree. It was here that he heard horse hooves pounding and metal clanking. A black stallion, wearing heavy armor, galloped past him. Zachary jumped out of the way. The horse caught a glimpse of him and slowed down, turning around. The massive equine's muscles rippled beneath his shiny, sweaty coat as he majestically trotted toward the young man. The horse stood in front of him, bowing his head. "Hello, Zachary. I am Cheva. Pleased to finally meet you."

"Hello...um...nice to meet you too."

Cheva raised his head and the armor clanked. He flicked his ears with irritation. "Could you do me a favor and get this off me?"

"Sure!"

The stallion kneeled, resting on the lush moss growing in the cool shade beneath the tree's massive canopy. His body armor pressed against the spongy, green carpet.

Zachary unhinged the flanged skirting that hung over the animal's front and hind quarters, pushing the metal covers off, then pulling the pins holding the neck plates, gently removing each one, releasing the horse's flowing mane. Then he undid the strap holding the shaffron, lifting it from the horse's head. He rested the saddle beside the tree.

The horse got up, shaking his mane. "Ah...this feels so much better! It's funny, the armor was meant for my protection, yet I only felt its limitations."

A man's voice echoed from deep in the woods, "Here, boy! Cheva!"

The horse's ears went back and his eyes narrowed.

Zachary asked, "You have an owner!? Why'd you let someone—"

Cheva interrupted, "I've been playing the part of dutiful servant, knowing that one day it would serve the purpose of meeting you."

"Wasn't there an easier way?"

"There's always an easier way, but we seldom see it at the time," Cheva answered introspectively.

The bushes rustled. Startled, Zachary turned. He saw a huge grizzly bear burst out of the dense shrubbery with Billy right behind him. Zachary was momentarily bewildered to see his friend. "How did you get here!?"

Billy laughed. "Old Indian trick!" He motioned with his hand to introduce his totem animal, "Everyone, meet Kaneonuskatew. Kane for short."

The bear put his paw over his round belly and bowed. "Pleased to meet you!"

53

Zachary was amazed at the bear's enormous size. "You're huge!"

The bear laughed, jiggling his belly. "Delightful boy."

Cheva said, "Pleased to meet you both. But now, I think it's time to take Zachary on a tour of the spirit realm. Would you care to join us?"

Billy answered, "I would be honored."

Kane lowered to all fours and the man sat on his back.

The bear grumbled, "You've put on weight."

"You're one to talk."

Cheva and Kane carried the two men through the age-old forest, past the giant oak trees towering over the elm, birch and underbrush. Zachary rode the horse bareback, holding onto the mane to steady himself. He reached out and plucked a leaf from a passing tree, admiring its texture, amazed at how real it seemed.

It wasn't long before they came across an old man sitting next to a stone table with a fire burning in its center. Behind him was a thatch-roof hut that was open in the front. The back wall was lined with wooden shelves holding earthen jars filled with herbs, seeds and dried roots. He motioned for them to sit with him, then sprinkled an herb into the fire. Zachary and Billy dismounted and sat down. Fragrant smoke drifted over them. With kind, wise eyes, the spirit guide looked at Zachary, asking, "Tell me, what is on your mind?"

"I want to save my parents' farm. Can you help?"

"Perhaps." The spirit guide sprinkled another herb over the flames. A plume of smoke rose up. "But first, I'd like you to do something for me."

"Okay," Zachary tentatively agreed.

54

"Imagine a mountain…"

"Okay…"

"Now imagine the mountain moving from one place to another." The spirit guide waited for Zachary to visualize it. "Did you see how easy that was?"

"Yes."

"Change your thoughts, change the world."

"You expect me to believe that the whole world will change for me!?" Zachary asked in disbelief.

"Change never impacts just one person. We are all connected."

"Like the Butterfly Effect?" Zachary glanced at Billy, who nodded in agreement, encouraging the young man to continue, "Well, change isn't always good. The world is getting worse."

The spirit guide explained, "The world is like a river with sludge lying at the bottom. On sunny days, the water appears to be clear and inviting, but inevitably, a storm comes along, forcing the sludge to the surface, muddying the water. When that happens, you become aware of it and perceive it as bad, but in reality, it is an opportunity to remove it…to heal it. If you don't, the sludge will settle to the bottom where it remains until the next storm comes along."

Billy lifted his hat to scratch his head. "Could we get a healing for the farm while we work on removing the sludge?"

"Yes, we can heal—"

"Great!" Zachary interrupted.

The spirit guide finished his thought, "We can heal the land, but please understand that if you don't heal yourself, you will continue relying on miracles to heal your manifestations, one after another, creating a cycle where you don't make any progress. Unless the root cause is eliminated, the problem will reappear, perhaps in the same form, perhaps in a different form."

"What good does it do to heal the land, if it'll just be ruined again?" Zachary complained. He was at a loss on how to proceed when a blue mist rolled across the ground. Curious, he and Billy turned around, mystified to see it flowing out of a blue door, slightly ajar.

The men and totem animals walked over to take a closer look, leaving the spirit guide behind.

Kane sniffed the door, then licked it, commenting, "Doesn't have much of a taste."

"You'll eat just about anything, won't you?" Billy asked.

Kane grinned. "You don't get a belly this big passing up opportunities!"

The small talk annoyed Zachary, who impatiently declared, "Obviously someone's heard our call. I need to save the farm! Let's see what's on the other side!"

"Look, I've got my doubts, but I'll go with you. If it doesn't work out, we can always come back here," Billy reasoned.

The blue door opened fully.

"Shall we?" Zachary asked Cheva.

The horse knelt so the young man could get on. He grabbed the horse's mane, riding tall, ready for a grand adventure as they strode through the mist. Billy and Kane followed closely behind them, disappearing behind the door.

CHAPTER 12

By the Sea

Several moons had passed since the intruders had devastated the tribe members' lives. Pahtia and Conchita quietly sat around the fire inside their hut, the flames reflecting in the shaman's worried, tired eyes. Conchita noticed, asking, "What is wrong, father?"

"I fear more intruders will come to finish the trail. I think we need to visit Maka once more. Will you come with me?"

"Of course."

He lit herbs to bless the journey and drive away the bad spirits, then he and Conchita closed their eyes, letting their spirits roam through a mystical rainforest teeming with exotic wildlife and birds. Pahtia looked around for his totem animal, surprised that the big cat wasn't waiting for him. "Taslia! Come! We need you!" A roar filled the air. Out of the mist, the black jaguar appeared. Pahtia said to her, "It is good to see you again," petting her head. "I need your help. Please take me to see Maka."

The sleek cat nodded, then strode through the dense jungle, guiding them to the waterfall.

Pahtia moved ahead, standing among the ferns at the water's edge where he beckoned his spirit guide. "Maka! Please come!" There was no answer. He called again, but she still did not appear. He called one more time before giving up. "Let us move on. Perhaps another spirit guide will hear our plea."

Taslia heeded his words, rising to her feet. She padded around the waterfall to a narrow staircase carved out of the mountainside, placing her large paw on the first step, leading them up the narrow, winding stairs.

They slowly ascended, one foot after the other. Once Conchita lost her footing, but then quickly regained it, causing stones to tumble down the steep walls. It was an arduous mode of travel, but one that eventually took them to great heights, offering a glorious view of the cliffs and shoreline below.

Around a bend, they came upon an old guru praying inside a cave. Pahtia hated to interrupt him, but felt his problem was urgent. He cleared his throat, hoping it would elicit a response, but the man did not flinch. After a moment, Pahtia said, "Excuse me. Can you help us?" The man remained motionless. Pahtia was unsure if he was being slighted or if the old guru was lost in concentration. Preferring not to know, he gestured for Taslia to continue up the stairs.

They arrived to a plateau overlooking the ocean. Waves crashed against the rocks below. Pahtia had never seen such a large body of water, but he didn't want to waste his time deciphering the unending sea—his only concern was to get rid of the intruders. "Will no one help us?" he lamented.

Conchita responded, "Father, someone will."

Taslia stated, "You are not asking for a healing, but for the death of an enemy. Are you sure you wish to meet the spirit who would grant this request?"

"Maka helped us last time. How is this different?"

"The intruders foolishly stayed. They could have left when the storm began, but greed clouded their judgment," Taslia explained, "This time you are asking for an outright attack."

"Our tribe has lived in the forest since time began. It is our home, our life. It is not theirs to take. The intruders have been warned. They have chosen death!"

A blue door landed with a thud behind them. Startled, Pahtia and Conchita spun around, watching the door swing open. A blue mist flowed across the ground toward them.

Taslia warned, "The answer you seek waits for you on the other side, but be careful what you wish for."

Pahtia boldly stepped through the doorway. Conchita and Taslia followed him.

59

CHAPTER 13

The Crystal Ball

The dragon followed Haruto through the blue door, emerging into total darkness except for the narrow pathway created by the luminous blue mist. He felt her unease as she trusted the vaporous trail to guide her. She suddenly stopped, looking behind her, simultaneously relieved and annoyed to see the dragon's silhouette highlighted by the glow of the blue mist. She confronted him, "Why are you following me?"

The dragon answered in a deep, rumbling voice, "Someone has to keep an eye on you."

Haruto suspected he had other motives, but her attention was diverted when she noticed that the mist behind the dragon was dissolving like a lit fuse. They needed to hurry or the path would disappear, leaving them stranded in the pitch-black void.

She ran ahead with her red cape billowing behind her. A light appeared in the distance peeking through a doorway. When Haruto reached it, she pushed the door open. On the other side was a grand, circular courtyard made of stone pavers set in a spiral pattern, built on a hilltop. In the middle was an enormous crystal ball perched on a marble pedestal.

Haruto and the dragon approached the glass sphere, fascinated by the blue mist swirling inside. Haruto strained to see what was hidden beneath the mist, but the harder she tried, the denser it became. The dragon flicked his forked tongue over the glass. His green, webbed wings were tucked back as he moved his horned head to and fro, curiously examining the crystal ball that he tapped with one of his sizable curved claws. He turned his head sideways, peering closely into the sphere with one of his golden eyes. "Nothing!" he grumbled, disappointed.

Another invisible door swung open. The Bear Claw First Nation members walked through the portal, examining their surroundings. They immediately noticed the woman wearing a red cape, who stood next to a dragon with smoke percolating out of his nostrils and glaring at them with his golden, reptilian eyes.

Chief Keme stayed near the door, wary of the beast. He called out to Haruto, "Are you a spirit guide?"

She shook her head, answering loudly, "No, I'm here looking for help."

The tribe members were disappointed. They wondered what to do next.

A third invisible door opened. Zachary and Billy made a grand entrance riding the black stallion and grizzly bear.

Billy jumped off his totem animal to approach the tribe, "Greetings, all my relations," offering his hand to Chief Keme.

The chief shook his hand. "It is good to meet you, brother. We came seeking help."

Billy responded, "We also seek help. Perhaps today, we'll find it." He proceeded to greet the rest of the tribe, but kept stealing glances at the beautiful Haruto guarded by the dragon.

Another invisible door swung open. Pahtia and Conchita entered the spirit realm, curiously observing the people who wore so many clothes. The black jaguar stepped through the door behind the pair, gracefully sitting down.

When Zachary caught sight of Conchita, he couldn't stop staring. She wore an animal-skin vest and sarong. Her exotic face was painted with a tribal design that accented her mesmerizing eyes. She followed her father across the courtyard where he introduced themselves to the others, "Greetings! I am Pahtia and this is my daughter Conchita. Are you spirit guides?"

Cecile Two Feathers shouted, "Another one!" Everyone groaned.

Pahtia didn't understand their reaction.

Chief Keme motioned for everyone to quiet down, "I am going to assume that we are all here for similar reasons. Perhaps one of the totem animals could lead us in the right direction?"

Cheva, Kane, Taslia and the dragon shook their heads. Taslia answered, "I'm out of my realm, literally."

A repetitive thundering sound was heard, as if an army of soldiers was marching toward them. A fifth invisible door opened. Mahakanta Suresh, the cotton farmer from India, led hundreds of thousands of spirits who advanced through the door.

Billy was shocked at the multitude. He asked Mahakanta, "Why are there so many of you?"

"We were farmers who planted magic seeds that ruined us. I am ashamed to say that each of us committed suicide after failing to provide for our families." His head hung low as he admitted, "Guilt gnaws at my heart for having left my children and wife with nothing."

Billy looked at the unending mass of farmer spirits flowing over the valley, their radiant, golden bodies shifting to and fro, swaying like wheat blowing in the wind. "What do you seek?" he asked.

"I do not know," Mahakanta answered solemnly. "Justice perhaps."

A shadow glided over the crowd, capturing everyone's attention. Overhead, an angel flapped his blue-tipped wings, softly landing on the courtyard. He had jet-black hair and pale skin that resembled translucent marble reflecting the clouds in the sky. He was stunningly handsome with a strong jaw line and piercing ultramarine eyes. Over his tall frame, he wore a sapphire-blue robe tied with a light-blue sash. The angel announced, "I am Bechard, Master of the Elements. I invited each of you here today to help you, as well as the planet, which is being destroyed by mankind's greed, corruption and indifference." He made his way to the crystal ball, waving his hand over it. The mist cleared, revealing the earth slowly rotating. Everyone gasped.

"Is that real?" Haruto asked, spellbound by its authentic resemblance.

Bechard smiled, "See for yourself."

Haruto stepped forward, searching for Japan, then her city of Fukushima. The image magnified, showing the nuclear plant and the workers who scrambled outside the facilities in their protective suits trying to contain the radioactive wastewater leaking out of control, spilling

63

into the boiling sea. She jumped back in horror. On the beach lay dead whales, sharks and porpoises. "Oh, my God! It's getting worse!"

Bechard responded, "Yes, it seems that mankind is constantly making blunders that are detrimental to its own health and the rest of the world."

Billy nudged Zachary, who was staring at Conchita, prompting him to step up to the crystal ball. They scanned the northeastern corner of the United States for the general vicinity of Pennsylvania.

"Should be there," Zachary said, pointing with his finger. The region came into view, displaying his family's farm, then the panorama shifted a mile to the east where the terrain was littered with active oil wells. "They know it's contaminating the water supply, yet they keep pumping!" he exclaimed, visibly upset.

"Let's move out of the way," Billy suggested.

Mahakanta stepped up to the globe searching for his beloved India. Former sights and smells flashed through his mind. He smiled remembering how vibrant India's culture had been for him. His dusty farm and vacant house appeared before the nearby city came into view. He saw his family begging on a street corner. "Oh, sweet devas, not my family! They are the lowest of low!" he cried, unable to watch any longer.

Zachary felt compassion for Mahakanta, putting his hand on his shoulder. The farmer dipped his head, crying. Pahtia and Conchita, who were heading toward the crystal ball, also stopped to comfort him.

Mahakanta lifted his head. With tears running down his face, he asked, "Have you ever been hungry while the earth seemed plentiful? Have you ever felt alone in a place filled with millions of people? I raised my arms to the heavens crying for help, but my plea fell on deaf ears. The world went on without me. It still ignores my family. How can this be? Does no one care?"

Zachary gently answered, "I'm sorry this happened to you."

Mahakanta stopped crying. "I can see clearly that the government should have stopped the sale of the magic seeds. So simple! The seed man showed me pictures of farms with bountiful crops, but now I know those farms had irrigation systems. Those seeds would never work for a small farmer like me. They knew that! But they didn't care."

No one knew what to say.

Conchita wanted to take her turn at the crystal ball, but hesitated to walk away from the distressed farmer. She watched the young man listening compassionately to Mahakanta. Zachary caught her stare. His green eyes penetrated her heart. She looked away, blushing. Her father noticed the chemistry between the two and quickly ushered Conchita away while glaring at the young man.

The father and daugher stood side by side gazing into the crystal ball, marveling at the Amazon rainforest's colorful vegetation, animals, birds and other creatures living in paradise. There were no signs of the intruders.

Pahtia sighed with relief, turning to leave, but Bechard stopped him, saying, "I think you need to see the immediate future." Time sped forward as day and night cycled inside the glass sphere until a convoy of armored SUVs and a bulldozer appeared, blazing a trail through the rainforest.

"What do they want!?" Pahtia asked angrily.

65

Bechard answered, "It is difficult to explain, but I will do my best. These people search for the earth's black blood, called oil, and other treasures, such as trees and animals. They take these things and exchange them for money. Money that is exchanged for other things."

"I do not understand. Is there not enough where they come from?" Pahtia couldn't comprehend the intruders' unquenchable thirst for the jungle's resources.

Billy said, "Let me try. When a person doesn't understand the ways of the Spirit, they feel empty, and they try to fill their emptiness with money, but it's never enough."

The shaman looked at Billy. He could tell this man had seen the outside world and knew things he would never know. "I do not understand this emptiness, nor do I want to. I just want the intruders gone," Pahtia said solemnly, holding his daughter close. From under her father's arm, Conchita shyly glanced at Zachary, finding him attractive despite his light skin and lanky build.

It was now the Bear Claw Tribe's turn to gaze into the crystal ball. Clustered together, they found Bear Claw Lake, watching it zoom closer until the oil disaster came into view. Black smoke hung over the land that was crisscrossed with fire channels. Wearing protective gear and oxygen tanks, firefighters sprayed foam over the flames, which kept reigniting because of the continual supply of crude oil oozing from the ground. The tribe's outrage intensified when they saw the devastation in living color.

Tom Running Deer cried out, "No! Not our precious land!" He struck the glass with his fist. Lightning shot out, coursing through the sky, striking the oil company's rigs and trucks, as well as the nearby military base's planes, vehicles and buildings.

Down below, the Falicon employees and Canadian soldiers were stunned. Without warning, lightning bolted in every direction. There was nowhere to hide. People cowered on the ground. A pilot opened his plane's door, falling to the pavement. Smoke rose from his head. His skin and clothes were blackened. Lightning struck an officer inside the air traffic control tower. He jerked back and forth as electricity tore through his body. Lightning filled the sky, continuing to strike until Tom removed his hand. He and the other tribe members were shocked, yet pleased, by the unexpected destruction.

Cecile reached over to touch the glass ball with her finger. A bolt of lightning hit one of the planes. The tribe members cheered.

Seizing the opportunity, Zachary ran to the glass ball, desperately searching for the oil rigs near his family's farm. When they spun into view, he lowered his fist onto the globe. Lightning erupted, striking the oil rigs below, sending a worker flying. The man hit the ground where he lay motionless. One of the gas storage units exploded.

Zachary was horrified. He had assumed the oil rigs were unmanned. *A man might be dead because of what I did,* he agonized.

Bechard waved his hand over the glass globe. The blue mist reappeared. "We need to be careful how we use this power. It's time to develop a plan.

After everyone had gathered around Bechard, he addressed them, "Let me begin with this thought, 'If you could solve your problems with no limitations of time, money or physics…how would you do it?'"

67

The question took the Bear Claw Tribe members by surprise. After feeling victimized for so long, it was hard for them to shift gears to feel empowered.

"Anything?" asked Cecile.

"Anything," Bechard assured her.

"Well, I'd stop the oil spill...and make the oil companies leave and never come back. In fact, disappear altogether. And then, I'd heal the land. Oh...and get our land back... the land the government stole from us."

"I think that sums it up," concurred Chief Keme. The other tribe members agreed.

Bechard looked at Haruto, "And you?"

"I want to stop the nuclear meltdown, and restore the land and sea, but at this point, it would take divine intervention."

"I think you will find all the power you need right here," Bechard offered, motioning with his hand.

Mahakanta shouted, "I want my life back! To live on the farm with my family, enjoying the fruits of our labor!"

Bechard nodded, then looked at Pahtia and Conchita, motioning for one of them to speak.

The shaman spoke, "Grave danger is heading toward our village. The intruders will come again, destroying the rainforest and my people. I want the intruders stopped forever!"

Zachary asked, "The stuff that happened in the glass ball. Did it actually happen?"

The fallen angel looked at everyone before him and said firmly, "Let me be very clear on this. Everything we do here in the spirit realm will manifest in the physical realm, which is why we need to be careful."

The Bear Claw Tribe members were especially happy with this news, because it meant that the oil company equipment and military base had been destroyed.

"Maybe we'll actually get our land back," Chief Keme commented.

"Who wants it now? It's all messed up!" Tom complained bitterly.

Bechard walked over to the glass ball, waving his hand over it. The mist dissipated, revealing the earth inside. "You know the old saying, 'oil and water don't mix?' Look closely."

Everyone watched the lake water spin around and around with such intensity that it became a waterspout, lifting the oil from the lake and washing it from the surrounding lifeless trees, offering it to the heavens. A wind swept down and gathered the oil, animal carcasses and tar balls, carrying the ravages of senseless human actions above the clouds. The water fell back into the lake, creating waves that flooded the forest, extinguished the flames, then slowly ebbed, returning to the lake. At the same time, the ground shook and trembled, shifting the land, filling in the cracks and crevices, sealing the oil below.

The Bear Claw Tribe members were amazed that the oil spill had been stopped, the water was clean and the fires were out. The lake and surrounding area looked fairly healthy, despite the dead plants and trees.

"Don't worry. The land will recover," Bechard assured them.

Chief Keme vigorously shook Bechard's hand. "Thank you!"

"You're welcome, but if you want to save the rest of the planet, we'll need as many people as possible. A group effort you might say. Is everyone in?"

They all nodded.

"Wonderful! Let's begin by inviting shamans from every corner of the earth!"

Inside the crystal ball, a remote Siberian tundra came into view. A shamaness hiked with two reindeer toward her cabin. Her multi-colored skirt flapped in the chilly wind. The reindeer obediently followed her inside where they rested on the dirt floor. She chopped wild carrots, adding them to the stew simmering over a fire, but stopped when she sensed a presence in her home. "Tell me, Spirit, what do you want?"

Bechard answered her telepathically, streaming the recent events through her mind.

She quickly grasped what they were trying to achieve and responded, "Nay, I prefer to be alone. People bring heartache."

"True enough!" Bechard agreed. "But how long before the oil companies trek across your land, destroying it with oil spills and pipelines?"

"Let me deal with it when the time comes."

"Why not put an end to it now? We can insist that the world use Earth-friendly solutions. And if we make our demands together, they won't be able to ignore us."

"Why don't you do it? You seem powerful enough."

"It's complicated," answered Bechard. "Let's just say there are universal laws that prevent me from interfering... too much. For this plan to work, it needs to be carried out, for the most part, by inhabitants such as yourself."

The shamaness pondered his words, then reluctantly said, "Feels like I'm dealing with the devil, but I'll work with you."

Bechard nodded, and then said, "We are honored to have you!"

CHAPTER 14

The Messengers

When Billy and Zachary returned from the spirit realm, the sun was low on the horizon. The forest cast eerie shadows and was filled with strange noises. A crow sat on a nearby branch observing them. The atmosphere agitated Zachary.

Billy studied the young man knowing the recent events were a lot for him to deal with, and it wasn't over. In Billy's hand was a rolled scroll tied with a blue ribbon that had materialized from the spirit realm.

Zachary asked, "Can I see it?"

Billy untied the ribbon. The ancient parchment unfurled, displaying a flourished message written in vibrant blue ink. Zachary studied the document a moment before pulling out his phone, snapping a picture of it.

"What do you plan to do with that?" Billy inquired.

"Every time I think I've lost my mind, I'm gonna look at this and know it's real."

"Well, let's send it on its way." Billy rolled the scroll back up, tied the blue ribbon around it, then held it above his head. The crow swooped down, snatching it with its feet. The men watched the bird fly above the trees and out of sight.

"Come on, kid, let's head back." Billy picked up his drum, slinging it over his shoulder.

They were almost out of the woods when Zachary asked, "What do you think about the lightning strikes? I mean...people are dead because of it. I feel really bad."

Billy didn't answer right away, contemplating his answer. "I don't like attacking anyone, but I'm not afraid to fight. You think innocent bystanders were killed, but each of us chooses his own destiny."

"I don't understand," said Zachary.

"Shit happens! The oil company employees and soldiers knew it was wrong—being paid to protect the selfish interests of a few old men. My father used to say, 'If you sleep with dogs, you're going to get fleas.'"

"But getting fleas is a long ways from being killed!"

"After you spend enough time in the spirit realm, you'll understand we don't die, we just change form. Those people aren't dead. They just don't have bodies at the moment."

"Not sure you're making me feel better."

"Wasn't trying to make you feel better, just understand, or at least see it from a different perspective."

Meanwhile, in Africa, a shaman wearing a multi-colored wrap stood outside his hut, resting on a gnarled-wood staff while holding a scroll tied with a blue ribbon above his head. A Bateleur eagle perched on the thatch roof cocked his head, then flapped his giant black and white wings, taking to flight, seizing the scroll out of the man's hand. The bird's giant wings stirred up the dusty ground as he ascended, flying toward the capital city of Kinshasa, located in the Democratic Republic of Congo.

In Siberia, the shamaness and her reindeer stood at the edge of a birch tree forest. A snowy-faced owl sat on a branch hooting, his round eyes staring at the old woman. As if on cue, he silently glided toward her, snatching the rolled parchment from her weathered hand.

73

CHAPTER 15

The Conspiracy Blogger

Norman P. Dunstead scoured the Internet looking for suspicious weather phenomena, UFO sightings and government cover-ups. He typed "strange weather" in the search bar. The top search result read, "BREAKING NEWS! Lightning Hits Canadian Military Base Near Oil Spill, Killing 3 Soldiers." He read the juicy details, complete with the first-ever photos of the Bear Claw Lake oil spill. Now that the air force base had been destroyed, there was no one on hand to prevent reporters from taking aerial shots and invading the property. The article quoted an anonymous firefighter as saying, "The lightning came out of nowhere! There wasn't a cloud in the sky." But the article also explained that, while unusual, lightning has been known to travel as far as 10 miles, striking people out of the blue on a sunny day.

Yeah, but this just happens to be over an oil spill, Norman countered, pondering the possibilities. *Weird military testing using its own facilities as Guinea pigs? Geo-engineering? Aliens?* Norman rested his chubby fingers on the keyboard trying to find the right words for his newest blog post.

Uninspired, he browsed the search results again. He found a news video that had just been posted in Alberta, Canada.

An attractive reporter spoke into her microphone, "This is Lisa Bantoné from Channel 5 News live at Bear Claw Lake reporting on the bizarre weather patterns we've been experiencing, which so far have included an earthquake, waterspout and a windstorm that literally swept away the oil spill that once covered this lake." The camera panned to show the healthier lake, although oil residue could still be seen on the tree trunks. "Combine these events with the lightning storm from earlier today, and you gotta admit, it's mighty strange. The locals claim the land is protected by the Bear Claw Tribe's ancestors taking revenge. At this point, I might believe anything," she said with a half smile. "Back to you, Gary."

Gary sat in the newsroom shaking his head in disbelief, "Wow! Incredible stuff, Lisa." He turned, looking directly into the camera, "We'll keep you informed of any changes in the situation, and of course, our condolences to the families of the fallen heroes. Now on to the news. Two men are dead after—" The video ended.

On to the news? Christ almighty! They should have 24-hour coverage at Bear Claw Lake. Who knows what'll happen there next? Norman thought. He began enthusiastically writing a blog post, complete with a video clip.

75

CHAPTER 16

Return to Bear Claw Lake

As soon as the Bear Claw Tribe members handed off the scroll, they headed toward the lake intending to verify that the oil spill had indeed been remedied. The young and old alike hiked through the woods carrying sacred totem objects and sage to cleanse the area of its negative energy. When they reached the lake, the people mourned for the dead plants and trees, but were relieved to discover that the oil was no longer gushing from the cracked reservoir. Finally, the land could heal.

Chief Keme led them in prayer, thanking the Great Spirit for bringing Bechard to them. After completing the prayers and burning the sage, the tribe trudged to the military base. As they drew near, the smoldering trucks and planes came into view. The base was abandoned except for the Channel 5 News crew, which was hurriedly packing up their equipment, trying to make it back to the station before dark. When they saw the Bear Claw Tribe emerge from the woods, the crew quickly unpacked the camera, rushing over to interview them.

Lisa held out her microphone. "What do you have to say about these recent events?" She waited for someone to speak, but the tribe members remained silent as they looked around assessing the damage.

A convoy of covered army trucks rumbled onto the base. As soon as the trucks stopped, soldiers jumped out. A Royal Canadian major shouted through a megaphone, "This is government property! All trespassers will be prosecuted! You must leave immediately! I repeat, you must leave immediately!"

The army's presence and demands reignited the tribe members' anger. Empowered by recent victories, the tribe stood its ground. The soldiers aimed their guns, advancing toward them, halting a short distance away. Some of the soldiers dropped to the pavement, propping their weapons, ready to shoot.

The Bear Claw Tribe had seen this all before, generation after generation, century after century. Tired of being displaced, abused and kicked around, they refused to obey.

"Leave or we'll shoot!" the major threatened.

Chief Keme weaved his way through the group, taking his place at the front to protect his people. He shouted, "We were here first! You stole our land, then destroyed it! You go home! Sail across the ocean, back to your ancestors. This is our land!"

One of the soldiers readied his gun, aiming through the scope.

Chief Keme instinctively jumped in front of Cecile just before the shot rang out. The bullet caught him in the heart. He crumpled to the ground.

"Hold your fire! Damnit! Put your guns down, NOW!"

yelled the major. "Somebody get a medic!"

Cecile wailed, "Noooo! Oh, God, no!"

Chief Keme's dead eyes stared blindly at the sunset. He had died on the land he loved—the land he had played on as a child. He had died a warrior.

The major demanded that the news crew turn off their camera and erase the footage, but it was too late. The live feed had already been transmitted to the station.

Cecile lay sobbing over Chief Keme's body. Others cried or grieved silently. A few raised their fists threatening to attack the soldiers.

A strong breeze rattled the leaves. Snowflakes carried by an arctic wind began falling. The flurry turned into a blizzard, leaving the soldiers confused and blinded by the instant snowstorm that fell short of the tribe, acting as a barrier between them.

Tom knelt by the chief, picking up his body, beginning the solemn journey home.

The tribe followed, vowing revenge.

CHAPTER 17

Zachary Returns Home

The day's events in the spirit realm weighed heavily on Zachary's mind as he parked the truck in the driveway. He noticed the light in the kitchen window and wondered if his parents were still up.

He slowly walked to the back of the house, entering the dimly lit kitchen. The dogs that had been sleeping under the table drowsily got up to greet him. His mother sat there gazing at nothing. Zachary quietly closed the door, waiting for her to notice him.

"We tested the soil," she said somberly, continuing to stare into space. "It's bad. The water is ruined." She looked at Zachary. "We can't drink it, or take a bath, or irrigate our crops."

Zachary saw the fear in her eyes. He walked over to her, bending to hug her. "It'll be all right."

Marilyn accepted his loving gesture. "I know."

She changed the subject. "Where have you been?"

"Out...with a friend."

"I hope you're staying out of trouble!"

Zachary hid his guilt. Everything he had been doing was to save the farm, but people had been killed and it troubled him deeply.

He went into the living room and turned on the television. A 24-hour news station displayed text that scrolled along the bottom of the screen, "Bear Claw First Nation Chief Killed by Canadian Army." Shocked, Zachary put his head in his hands, unsure of what to think or feel.

Marilyn noticed her son's reaction and came over to sit by him. "What's the matter, Zachary? Tell me what's wrong."

"A friend died today."

"Who!? What are you talking about?" She glanced at the TV screen.

"Chief Keme died."

"I don't understand. Who's the chief? How did you know him? Does this have something to do with your new friend?"

"Yes, I met Chief Keme because of Billy."

"Zachary, you need to be careful! I don't want you getting hurt with radical stuff. It's easy to get caught up in a cause."

"Mom, that's the problem! Nobody's getting caught up in anything."

"Zach, listen to me. Promise me you won't get involved with these radical groups. You might get killed!"

He felt the fear in her heart. Nobody loved him more than his mother and he didn't want to upset her, but he also didn't want to lie to her. "How can you ask me to do nothing after the oil company destroyed our land and the government turns a blind eye?"

"It's not fair!" Marilyn shouted, surprised at her own anger. She calmed down. "It's not fair and I would love to take down the oil companies and corrupt politicians, but at some point, I just want to be happy. I don't want to spend my life fighting." She stroked her son's head, brushing his hair to the side. "I want to enjoy the rest of my life *with you in it*. Please be careful."

The moon shone between the clouds. An owl hooted from a nearby branch. Billy sat on a tree stump beside the small fire he had built. A light glowed inside his trailer. The dog warmed himself next to the flames, resting his head on his forepaws. Billy sprinkled tobacco over the fire, watching the smoke curl into the dark sky. He prayed, "Ancestors, a great warrior died today. Please welcome this brave man into your loving arms." He sprinkled more tobacco into the fire. "Chief Keme, you are a good man. We'll continue the fight in your honor." He raised his beer toasting the chief, "It was a good day to die. Peaceful journeys!"

 The owl hooted as if saying, "Amen," and the crickets offered their condolences, chirping softly in the darkness.

81

CHAPTER 18

The Crow

A crow flew over the horizon tightly clutching a scroll in its claws. The expansive, well-manicured lawn of the White House came into view where the president and the first lady were being prepped for an interview showcasing their organic garden. The couple wore blue jeans and plaid shirts to fit the part. A makeup artist finished touching up the president's foundation.

The famous television reporter, Barbara Phillips, approached the president and his wife. "We'd like to get some candid footage of you two working together in the garden, right after we ask you a few questions. Is that okay?"

"Of course, Barbara. We'd love to show the American people how important the environment and healthy living are to us—"

Barbara interrupted, "Excuse me, Mr. President, but we weren't rolling yet. Could you save that and start over?"

"Certainly. We'd love to show the American people how important the environment and healthy—"

The crow swooped into the scene, fluttering over the president, dropping the scroll on his lap before flying away, cawing loudly. The president stared at the scroll, afraid to touch it. He jumped up. The rolled parchment fell on the grass. The first lady sat stunned.

A Secret Service agent rushed over to examine it, holding his arm up protectively toward the president. "Stand back, sir! It could be laced with something!"

Moments later, an official-looking man arrived on the scene wearing gloves and carrying a plastic bag. He cautiously used tongs to pick up the scroll, stating, "We'll have it examined and get back to you with the results, Mr. President."

"Let me know as soon as you find out anything," the president instructed, trying to keep his cool. He looked at the reporter. "Sorry for the interruption, but I need to change my clothes." He stopped walking mid-step. "Oh, Barbara, let's make sure that footage doesn't appear anywhere. Understood?"

"Of course, sir!" She glanced at the cameraman. "Erase it."

He nodded, hitting a button.

CHAPTER 19

The Scroll's Message

Later that afternoon while the US president was enjoying a cup of coffee in the Oval Office, his secretary announced that the head of the Secret Service was on the phone.

The president hit the speaker button. "Ted, you got the test results?"

"Yes. No toxins, viruses or any chemical considered dangerous." The president sighed with relief. The head of the Secret Service continued, "However, because of the unusual circumstances, I thought you might want to read it. The scroll that is."

"Sounds good. Send it over. I'll take a look."

An hour later, an internal courier delivered a copy secured in a black leather attaché case, laying it on the desk. The president was busy talking with his staff and barely noticed its arrival.

It wasn't until later, when the president was in the middle of a private conversation with his chief counsel, that he remembered the scroll. He said to the lawyer, "An interesting thing happened this morning. I'm outside doing one of those bullshit photo ops with my wife. God, she loves those things. Anyway, a bird drops a scroll on my lap—"

"Excuse me, a bird!?"

"Yeah, strangest thing. Anyway, the scroll's here. Would you like to see it?"

"Sure. This should be interesting."

The president went to his desk and opened the attaché case. Inside was a copy of the scroll printed on multiple letter-sized sheets. The men stood side by side reading it.

This directive is intended for the President of the United States and all members of its government, sent on behalf of Earth who cannot speak for herself.

This letter serves as fair warning that if the following terms are not met there will be consequences:

1. You will phase out the use of energy sources that are not renewable and/or harmful to the environment, such as oil, natural gas, shoal fracking, dams and nuclear power. Within seven years, only Earth-friendly technology may be used for energy needs, which do not harm the environment during the process of collecting, installing, using or disposal.

2. The use, testing and selling of genetically modified organisms (GMO) shall cease immediately. A trust fund shall be established to compensate farmers of GMO crop failures, as well as those who were unable to sell their crops after being classified as GMO. This applies to any and all farmers throughout the world, including farmers whose crops were contaminated by neighboring GMO fields.

3. Use, storage and/or ownership of nuclear weapons is prohibited. These weapons must be dismantled immediately.

4. The use of natural or synthetic chemicals to kill any living creature, vegetation or human is prohibited, i.e. pesticides, herbicides, neurological chemicals, systemics, etc. The ownership of such chemicals will be considered a violation. You have one year to properly dispose of them in such a way that they do not contaminate the environment.

5. The production of non-biodegradable plastic is to cease within one year. The only exception is medical equipment and supplies.

6. You must humanely raise farm/commercial mammals/birds/fish and treat them with respect. All animals and birds must be kept in spacious facilities that are well-maintained, well-ventilated and allow ample room for them to move freely. All animals and birds shall have access to open-air areas. All fish farms are to provide ample swimming areas. All farms are to install video cameras that allow public viewing of interaction between humans and animals to prevent cruelty. All feed must be compatible with their natural diets. None of the animals, birds or fish are to be given hormones, steroids or chemicals. Antibiotics can be used to treat current illnesses, but not for prevention. All slaughtering processes are to be humane with no pain or emotional suffering.

7. Pollution is to be reduced by 70% within seven years.

8. Only existing managed forests may be harvested. Existing farmland may be converted into managed forests. Trees in virgin forests cannot be cut for commercial purposes. Trees can be cut for forest management and forest fire prevention; however, all the trees (except diseased) that are cut in virgin forests are to remain within the forest, providing nutrients for the vegetation, as well as homes for the animals.

9. You will set up recycling plants in every city.

10. Weather warfare and geo-engineering, such as chemtrails, are prohibited and shall cease immediately. To help restore balance in nature, commission your indigenous people to actively work with the weather spirits.

This message has been delivered to government leaders throughout the world. All leaders are expected to work together to develop solutions and publicly share those solutions within thirty (30) days.

As a display of power, we recently stopped the oil spill at Bear Claw Lake in Alberta, Canada, relocating the oil waste and casualties to the Canadian parliamentary complex in Ottawa, Ontario.

Respectfully,
Earth Sentinels

Oh, God, another nut, thought the president.

The lawyer said, "Seems like a tall order." He chuckled.

The president scowled. "No nuclear weapons? Phase out oil? Impossible. Weather spirits? Ridiculous."

"You could probably do number six—"

"First, I am not doing anything. Second, this obviously came from someone who needs help."

"What's that at the bottom?" the lawyer asked.

"Earth Sentinels?"

"No, here." He pointed at the last sentence. "Where it says they stopped the oil spill at Bear Claw Lake, relocating the oil to Ontario. I didn't know that happened."

"As far as I know, it hasn't," replied the president.

They were both right. The oil was being carried by the wind and wouldn't drop onto the Canadian complex until morning.

CHAPTER 20

Haruto's Choice

Haruto was meditating in the garden under an old cherry tree where moss grew on the shaded rocks nestled between its roots.

The Voice whispered to her, "Haruto...who have you been listening to?"

What do you mean? she thought, perplexed.

"The lightning strikes...the dead men," the Voice reminded her. "These were not loving acts."

We had to do something! Haruto bitterly ruminated that the government did not fully comprehend the damage caused by the ongoing Fukushima disaster. Right after the meltdown first occurred, the politicians proposed building a new nuclear plant, relinquishing the idea only after massive protests by the Japanese people. *Rebuild? Had they learned nothing from history?* She recalled the United States dropping atomic bombs on Hiroshima and Nagasaki during World War II. Nine years later, the US accidentally radiated a Japanese fishing boat while testing a hydrogen bomb in the Pacific. The fishermen returned to shore, sold their contaminated fish, and then developed acute radiation sickness. In an effort to mend fences, President Eisenhower compensated the fishermen and built the nuclear reactor in Fukushima. He dubbed the gift, "Atoms for Peace."

She wondered, *What could possibly be going through their minds? What draws Japan to nuclear catastrophes like a moth to a flame? What karmic lessons are they doomed to repeat, over and over again, until they learn from their mistakes?*

"Still examining the darkness, little one?" the Voice asked.

No! I'm done. We will fix this problem and put an end to this stupidity!

"Ask yourself if what you are doing is loving."

It's loving to the planet, she countered.

The Voice suggested, "Why don't we visit the shoreline near the nuclear plant?"

Haruto agreed. Instantly her spirit floated over the beach where she viewed the bloated carcasses of whales, sharks, dolphins and fish. The stench was overpowering. She gagged, desperate to get away until she noticed the spiritual essences rising out of the dead marine mammals and fish, swimming happily in the air around her. Haruto's long, black hair began streaming in an invisible current and her clothes billowed as if she were under water. Playful dolphin spirits frolicked through the mystical sea while energetic shark bodies circled on the surface over the slow-moving, gigantic whales. Translucent fish darted in schools around her. Haruto embraced the love and unity among their souls, feeling her heart soar, but then she glimpsed the nuclear plant, causing her joy to screech to a halt.

The Voice advised her, "It's your choice. Which do you prefer to see?"

90

Haruto beheld the spirits frolicking around her, then viewed the nuclear plant again, becoming enraged by the steam rising off the boiling sea while workers in bio-hazard suits moved about the facilities. "It's not right! They can't do this!" she yelled, clenching her fists.

The spirits faded away. Haruto found herself once again sitting in the garden. She immediately regretted letting her fear take over, shouting, "I chose wrongly!"

The Voice spoke to her, but Haruto couldn't hear It. Her anger and regret blocked it.

She felt utterly alone until she remembered the spirit guides—the samurai soldiers, crone and priestess—who might help her. Breathing deeply, she closed her eyes, letting her spirit roam free. Clouds rolled in.

The dragon appeared, examining Haruto with his golden eyes. His voice rumbled as he said, "Ah, I see you have returned. Very well, follow me." He led the way, his large frame lumbering through the mist. Once more, they came to the ornate iron gate, moving past it, entering the forest where eventually they met the spirit guides, who were relaxing around the fire pit.

The samurai soldiers and priestess stood to bow, pleased to see the Miko again. Haruto returned the bow.

The crone who remained sitting, heckled, "Back again, heh?"

The priestess motioned for Haruto to join them by the fire. "Tell us what is on your mind."

Haruto confided, "I'm frustrated. I don't understand why my desire to heal a disaster is having such a negative response."

"There's nothing wrong with trying to help. It's how and why you do it that matters. Learn how to love the spirit behind these events and the events will respond to your love, transforming themselves."

Haruto was unsure. "Hmmm...let me ask you this, 'How can the nuclear disaster be fixed?'"

The priestess smiled. "That is easy. Forgive it. Through forgiveness, you reinforce our oneness, our perfection, and refuse to be deceived by outward appearances."

Haruto felt her resistance to this advice welling up. How she wished she could let her anger go.

"Remember, you are never angry for the reason you think you are..." the priestess said as her voice faded away.

Everything went black. Haruto opened her eyes. The sun was setting. A chill was in the air and the garden walls cast long shadows across the ground. Shivering, she followed the path back to the temple.

CHAPTER 21

Conchita

In the rainforest, water softly dripped from the moist vegetation. Most of the tribe members were napping to avoid the mid-day heat. Sitting inside a hut, Conchita played peekaboo with the baby Capuchin monkey that popped its head up from under the arm of its surrogate mother, Sonsala, who was breastfeeding her baby. The well-fed monkey hid its head again. Conchita giggled, then asked Sonsala, "Have you named this one yet?"

"Her name is Bebe. A good monkey, but hopefully, she and the older one will return to the forest where they belong." Sonsala petted the creature on the head. Bebe drowsily closed her eyes, enjoying the attention. "Why don't we see if the monkeys remember each other?" Sonsala suddenly stood up, carrying a baby in each arm.

They strode across the common area and entered the hut where the adult Capuchin lay recuperating. Although still weak from his injuries, the monkey's eyes lit up when he saw a familiar face. He raised his arm, beckoning Bebe. The little one was curious, but afraid to let go of the woman who had given her a second chance at life. Sonsala set the baby monkey on the ground, nudging her toward the male monkey. Bebe hesitantly walked over to him. He tenderly reached out, stroking her head. She smelled his arm, remembering him, touching the scar on his face, tracing it with her fingers.

As Sonsala watched the two monkeys interact, she mentioned, "The women like him. He is a good patient. Never bites!" Sonsala's own infant began to fuss. She soothed him, then said, "Tawka likes you. Maybe you will get married and have babies?"

Conchita was torn. She had thought Tawka would make a great husband until she met the pale outsider with green eyes, who was always on her mind. *Does his skin feel the same as mine? Can he climb a tree as well as the other men? Can he stealthily move through the forest?* But her most prominent thought was, *Does he like me?* "Who knows what tomorrow brings," she replied, avoiding the question.

"You will break the heart of Tawka if you do not marry him."

I need to be happy, too, Conchita thought, *but how would the pale outsider and I ever be together? I would never be able to live apart from the rainforest and he would not want to live here.*

CHAPTER 22

Analyzing the Scroll

The CIA director entered the US president's office. "Good morning, sir. I have a delicate matter to discuss with you."

The president crossed his arms. "Have a seat. What's on your mind?"

Frank said, "It's the scroll, the one delivered weeks ago. We've done our homework and here's what we know. The parchment is 2,000 years old—highly valuable in its own right. The blue ink is the same type used in Egyptian tombs. The ribbon is ancient silk from China, carbon dated at 600 BC."

The president interjected, "So we're not dealing with a half-ass job."

"No, sir, it appears that someone with means has taken the time to create a rather expensive message. Our informants have spoken with the other leaders, and it seems they've received the same message on the same paper, tied with ribbon cut from the same cloth. All delivered by birds. More important, the weather phenomenon mentioned in the letter—those events can't be explained."

Frank removed several photographs from his briefcase, spreading them over the coffee table. "The oil from this location," he pointed to a photograph of Bear Claw Lake, "ended up here." He slid another photo closer to the president, who picked it up, examining an aerial shot of the Centre Block building in Ontario covered in oil.

"When you consider the timing, method and recent events, we have to consider the possibility that we're dealing with supernatural forces," Frank stated, waiting for the commander in chief to digest the information. "You know, we have a program that deals with this sort of activity."

The president nodded. "I've heard rumors, but thought it was shut down."

"Nope. It's still alive and well," Frank responded.

"What are you suggesting?" asked the president.

"I'd like one of our psychics to see what he or she can pick up, but there are some drawbacks." Frank paused, waiting for a reaction, but the president simply stared back at him, so he continued, "It'll be difficult to hide our snooping when the 'people' we're snooping on," he used his fingers to indicate the quotes around the word 'people,' "are highly attuned."

"You mean they'll know we're snooping?" the president clarified.

"Most likely, and if we're caught, they might provide false data or worse."

"Hmmm. Well, why don't you have someone give it a try. See what they come up with. But let's keep this between us. Okay, Frank?"

He nodded.

CHAPTER 23

Let the Storms Begin

Thirty days had passed since the scrolls were delivered, and now it was time for the Earth Sentinels to discuss the world's response. Bechard stood near the crystal ball with his blue-tipped wings folded back and hands clasped as he patiently waited for everyone to arrive.

The original members—Billy, Zachary, the Bear Claw Tribe members, Haruto, Pahtia and Conchita—sat on stone benches in the center court while their totem animals waited nearby.

Conchita gazed at Zachary. He felt her stare and looked at her. She smiled shyly, then lowered her eyes. He unconsciously puffed out his chest.

Haruto lounged on a bench by herself smoking a slender pipe. The fierce-looking dragon settled behind her, resting his forepaws on the stone seat.

Mahakanta stood on the courtyard. Behind him were hundreds of thousands of kindred spirits, spilling over the courtyard and across the valley.

The other members appeared, one after another.

Medicine men and women, shamans, Miko, Shinto, mudangs, Ngakpas, Jhakri, Noro, klong folk, Alignalghi, Sangomas, Hatałii, curanderos, and Machi from around the world entered the spirit realm through the invisible doors.

When they all had taken their places, Bechard raised his arms, greeting them. "As you know, it has been thirty days with no response to our demands. While not surprising, it is disappointing." The Earth Sentinels nodded their heads. "But before we go any further, I want to honor Chief Keme, who was killed by the Canadian Army."

Some of the members who weren't aware that he was dead gasped while the others lowered their heads in recognition of their loss.

They were all startled when a voice called out, "Hey! I'm not dead!" Chief Keme appeared in the center of the courtyard next to Bechard. The chief was no longer covered in blood, instead, he appeared young and strong, wearing a traditional, fringed buckskin shirt and pants embroidered with colorful beads in geometric shapes. He arched his back and raised his arms, shouting, "I might not be earthbound, but I'm alive!"

The crowd cheered.

Cecile ran over to tightly hug him, crying tears of joy. The other tribe members rushed to greet him.

Zachary felt his heart expand, wondering what there was to fear, if there was no death.

Mahakanta waited until everyone embraced the chief, then approached him, asking, "How can you be so happy? You were murdered!" A hush fell over the courtyard. Everyone waited for Chief Keme's response.

"I died a warrior! With my head held high, defending

my tribe. Now I commune with my ancestors, and one day will be reunited with my family and friends here in the spirit realm. There is no sorrow. I am never alone!" He then posed his own question, "Why aren't you happy?"

Mahakanta lowered his head. Tears ran down his face. "I was a fool..." he couldn't finish his sentence. The farmer spirits gathered around him, comforting him.

Bechard didn't want the meeting to drown in sorrow, so to divert the crowd's attention, he patted the chief on the back, loudly saying, "Let's hear it for Chief Keme!" The members cheered. "Now on to our agenda of saving Earth! As you know, the world's leaders have ignored our demands. To get their attention, we will have to increase our display of power, and I have an idea that is fairly harmless, but a huge inconvenience to our *fine* world leaders." Bechard had a devilish smile on his face.

"I propose we create storms over governmental headquarters. To achieve this, each of you will stand next to the crystal ball and find the capitol, palace or headquarters of your country, then touch the glass while repeating this intention...'Thirty days and nights, rain and lightning strikes.'" He added, "If you live in a country with states or provinces, do those as well—" The fallen angel suddenly stopped talking, peering to the side. A presence stood among them, but the shadowy silhouette disappeared when it realized it had been discovered. Most of the group missed seeing the murky figure and wondered what was going on. "It seems we've been compromised by an uninvited visitor," Bechard informed them. "We will need to be more careful in the future. No matter...the spy has left. So back to my proposal. Does anyone object to creating the storms?" He waited a moment, but when no one disagreed, he proclaimed, "Let's begin!"

Zachary and Billy approached the crystal ball, easily finding the United States. The nation's Capitol zoomed to the surface. Billy touched the glass while reciting, "Thirty days and nights, rain and lightning strikes."

Rain began pouring over the domed building and its circular lawn. The rain steadily increased until it was coming down in buckets. Lightning flared over the neatly groomed grounds. The tourists ran for cover as lightning struck the bronze statues of embodied heroes and zapped the light posts and flagpoles. Sparks flew everywhere. When the drenched tourists reached the street, they were surprised to be greeted by sunshine and dry pavement. They looked back in amazement realizing the storm was perfectly contained, as if held behind an invisible wall. Onlookers circled the Capitol studying the storm.

It took a while for the Billy and Zachary to set the intentions over all of the state capitols, but when done, they stood back admiring their handiwork, then got out of the way, allowing the others to step forward.

The President of the United States was eating breakfast with his wife and two young daughters in the private dining room at the White House, a mile-and-a-half from the nation's Capitol. In the distance, thunder rumbled and lightning flashed. His daughters stopped eating to peer out the window.

The first lady wiped her mouth with a napkin, commenting, "Sounds like a storm's coming."

The president nodded absentmindedly. The red phone on the curio rang. He answered it, listening to an urgent message, then tossed his napkin on the table, saying to his wife, "I need to check on a few things."

He walked down the hallway, stepping into the elevator, heading down.

When the wood-clad doors slid open, two assistants were waiting to greet him. They walked briskly beside the president, ready to brief him on the day's agenda.

His executive assistant, Kristina Burns, did her best to keep up with the president, although her short legs were no match for his. "Mr. President, the first thing, and maybe the only thing, we need to address today is the storm over the Capitol."

"Is it headed our way?"

Kristina realized the president was unaware of the situation. "Sir, the storm is *only* over the Capitol."

The president stopped in his tracks. He was going to ask something, but thought better of it. Instead, he walked into the Oval Office, immediately going to the window where he saw the isolated storm in the distance.

Deeply concerned, he turned on the television, flipping through the stations until he found a live feed of Channel 9's weekday reporter, Mark Johnson. A caption across the bottom of the screen read, "Freak Storm Over US Capitol."

The handsome reporter appeared mid-sentence, "—unnerving, isn't it? What makes the storm so unusual is it's only over the US Capitol building! I've been standing here five minutes and I'm completely dry!" True to Mark's word, not a hair was out of place on his well-groomed head. The reporter paused, pressing his hand to his earpiece. "This just in. It seems other capitols throughout the US are experiencing the same thing! Unbelievable!" Mark began repeating the newsfeed streaming through his earpiece, "Michigan, New York, Virginia, Florida, Kentucky, Pennsylvania...Oh, my God! It appears every capitol building is having the same thing. What does this mean!? It can't be good."

The president hit the remote, shutting off the TV. He

picked up the phone and called the CIA director. "Hello, Frank, want to tell me what's going on?"

"Mr. President, just got this. You remember that program I mentioned last time we spoke?"

"Yes."

"Well, one of our guys was able to penetrate the Earth Sentinels' meeting this morning and overheard them planning these storms."

"You're saying they created them?"

"Yes, sir, it seems that way."

"Did your guy find out how long these storms will last?"

"Thirty days."

"What!? How are we going to explain this to the American people? I need my advisors! Get here as soon as you can!" The president hung up, then directed his assistant, "Set up a meeting with my top chiefs ASAP!"

Lightning crackled through the sky. An enormous boom of thunder shook the windows. The president winced.

State Senator George Stanmond III prided himself on being the first to arrive at the Louisiana State capitol every morning, but today, his work ethic had bitten him in the butt. He had arrived before the supernatural storm started and was now stuck inside wistfully staring out the main entrance waiting for his assistant to arrive.

The senator used his cell phone. "Donny, you close?"

"Sir, I'm pulling up now. Be there in a sec." Donny had worked for the senator for 14 years picking up the senator's breakfast, dry cleaning and even buying gifts for his family, but navigating through a supernatural storm was the ultimate sacrifice he had performed to date.

Donny stopped his SUV on the street in front of the

capitol, putting the car in reverse, slowly backing over the curb, entering the storm. The rain was deafening as it pounded on the rooftop. He turned on the front and rear windshield wipers, straining to see through the rearview mirror as he carefully drove down the wide sidewalk backwards. When the back tires bumped the entrance steps, he stopped, then pushed a button. The hatch opened.

The senator was a large man with a wide girth, who hadn't sprinted in quite a while. George made a mental note not to rush too fast—afraid he might slip on the stairs, but on the other hand, he needed to move quickly to avoid being hit by lightning.

The nervous driver honked, prompting the senator to hurry. George braced himself before flinging the door open, rushing over the landing and down the stone steps. He was soaked before he leaped into the back of the vehicle, which sank under his weight. George slipped on the rubber mat when he unsuccessfully tried to close the hatch. Lightning hit a streetlight, scaring Donny who stomped on the gas pedal, peeling down the sidewalk, nearly losing the senator out the back. At the edge of the courtyard, the SUV cut through the shield of rain, dropping off the curb, bouncing George in the air. Donny hit the brakes, coming to a standstill on the dry pavement. The senator slammed against the backseat. The driver sat in shock watching the rapidly moving wipers squeak across the dry windshield.

The wet, frazzled senator wormed his way out of the cargo area, walking around the vehicle to sit in the passenger seat with water dripping down his face. His hair, which had been strategically placed over his bald spot, was now strung across his face. "Thanks, Donny. I owe you one," he said, combing his hair with his fingers, trying to regain some of his dignity. He studied the capitol barely visible through the heavy rain. "This can't be good."

Elsewhere, in Moscow, Russia, cafés served hot chocolate, tea and coffee to the patrons trying to escape the chilly night. No one dared go near the darkened Kremlin complex, which was cursed with lightning and rain.

The Russian president sat in his den, staring at the flames in the fireplace as he downed a shot of vodka. He swallowed hard, thinking, *Somehow, someway, this is America's fault.*

The stark-white Democratic Republic of the Congo capitol sat vacant as the metaphysical lightning storm pummeled it, forcing the prime minister to conduct business with parliament members out of his home where they exchanged heated debates regarding what to tell the city's eight million inhabitants whose fears ran high, because they attributed the eerie storm to witchcraft.

After everyone left, the prime minister sighed, waiting for the shaman to arrive. Deep in the heart of Africa, political leaders unofficially hired shamans to help them gain and retain their power. Here, it was unthinkable to separate the spiritual from the political.

A butler appeared at the doorway of the dining room. The prime minister sat at the 14-foot teakwood dining table surrounded by curved-back chairs. Lion, rhino, tiger and antelope stuffed heads were mounted to the walls on each side of the glass cabinet filled with priceless artifacts. "There is someone here to see you, sir," the servant announced.

"Please show him in," the prime minister requested without bothering to ask who it was. The butler nodded, leaving to retrieve the visitor.

The shaman was heard coming down the hall, his wooden staff hitting the polished hardwood floor. He stopped at the dining room entryway, waiting for his presence to be acknowledged.

The prime minister walked over to greet him, a courtesy usually reserved for high officials. "Please have a seat," he requested cordially, "Would you like something to drink?"

"Water would be excellent," the shaman answered, taking his place on one of the comfortable chairs, adjusting his multi-colored wrap, happy to rest after his long journey.

The men made small talk while the butler served their drinks. "Will there be anything else, sir?"

"No, thank you," the prime minister answered.

The butler closed the door on his way out.

"Tell me what is going on," requested the prime minister.

The shaman brought up the confidential topic, "You received a scroll, did you not?"

The president nodded his head.

"And you ignored the message."

"Yes, because the demands were ridiculous! Our country can't stop using oil! Plus, I'll not have some radical group dictating this country's future. If these Earth Sentinels have something to say, they can do it publicly."

The prime minister waited for the shaman to respond, but the spiritual leader kept sipping his water. Slowly, it dawned on the prime minister that he was doing the same thing— plotting behind closed doors. He half smiled, amused by his own hypocrisy, "Can you meet these Earth Sentinels? See if we can work out a reasonable deal? If they want to protect the earth...that's a good thing. Surely, we can work together."

The shaman smiled, then took another sip of water.

CHAPTER 24

Emergency Meeting

In response to the bizarre storms, the US president ordered an emergency meeting with his top advisors and the CIA director at the White House. They sat in the darkened Press Briefing Room taking advantage of its high-tech capabilities.

"To get things up to speed," the president said, "why don't you take the lead, Frank? Share what's happened so far."

"Sure. Be glad to." Frank clicked the remote in his hand. A world map appeared on the screen. "Each red dot marks the location of a paranormal storm. The storms are consistent—lightning and heavy rain over government headquarters." He clicked the remote. A photo of the scroll appeared. "Approximately thirty days ago, world leaders received a list of demands written on scrolls exactly like this one. Same paper, ribbon and ink, all signed 'Earth Sentinels.'" He used his red laser to point out the name at the bottom of the scroll. "Here's where it gets really weird... each scroll was delivered by a bird." The advisors looked at him as if he was crazy, but Frank persevered, "Believing we might be dealing with the metaphysical, we enlisted a psychic to penetrate the group, and he overheard the Earth Sentinels plotting these storms before they occurred. So, I guess what I'm saying is...we're fairly confident we're dealing with supernatural powers."

The men sat dumbfounded. No one wanted to be the first to acknowledge they believed unearthly forces existed. Various advisors crossed and uncrossed their arms while others squirmed in their seats. Several started to say something, then changed their minds, snapping their mouths closed.

"All right, everyone, I know this isn't easy, but we need a plan!" the president demanded.

Frank cleared his throat. "Why don't we bring in the psychic who infiltrated the Earth Sentinels? He's experienced with this kind of thing."

Most nodded, relieved.

The president instructed, "Bring him in. We'll resume after lunch."

The advisors had eaten in the Cabinet Room and were nervously killing time sipping coffee. A buzzer sounded, followed by a woman's voice announcing, "Mr. President, there's a visitor here to see you, accompanied by CIA Special Agent Ryan Foremost."

"Send them in, please." The president set down his coffee.

Agent Ryan escorted the psychic, Max Jones, into the room, introducing him to the president and advisors who stood to greet the tall man wearing a tie-dyed shirt and blue jeans.

"Good to meet you, Max," the president said, shaking his hand. "Please have a seat." He looked at Frank. "Why don't you take the lead on this one?"

"Sure, Mr. President." Frank turned his attention toward Max. "Could you please tell us what you know?"

Max surveyed the room filled with the world's top-ranking advisors, who were staring at him, waiting to hear what he had to say. "Well, I saw an angel. He was the leader. And spirits, lots of spirits...hundreds of thousands of them!"

The advisors sat back in their seats trying to comprehend the enormity of the enemy's ranks and accept the possibility of supernatural forces.

Frank asked, "By spirits, do you mean that the Earth Sentinels are not of this world?"

"I'm not sure. The angel isn't, but it's possible some of the spirits have physical bodies here on earth. They could have been visiting the spirit realm on a temporary basis, much like I was."

"So, it's possible some of them might have a weak link, physical bodies, we could get a hold of."

"Yeah, I heard one man's name—Chief Keme."

A senior advisor mentioned, "Isn't that the name of the Indian shot by the Canadians?"

"But he's dead," the Chief of Staff interjected.

"Were any members of the chief's tribe there?" Frank asked Max, then clarified, "In the spirit realm, I mean."

"Yes, now I remember. There were a dozen of them. A woman and the rest were men...most likely the tribe's elders."

Frank pondered this information "Would it be possible for you to return and discover the identities of the Earth Sentinels?"

"I'm not sure. The angel noticed me last time and will be on guard."

"Tell us more about this angel. Does he have a name?"

"I didn't hear his name, but I did some research. I believe he's the fallen angel Bechard, Master of the Elements."

The men scoffed under their breath.

An advisor piped up, "Fallen angel? Isn't that a demon?"

"Well, technically yes, but they're not all trying to steal your soul. Some are like us, simply experiencing the world."

"But with *magical* powers," quipped one of the advisors.

The others chuckled.

"Yes," Max confirmed, slightly embarrassed.

The president was annoyed by the roving conversation, interrupting them, "Men, we need to explore all possibilities. If Max can infiltrate the group and get more information, we should support him." He asked Max, "Think you can get back in there?"

Max was uncertain. "Mr. President, I can try."

"National security depends on you being able to do this. Don't just try. Do it!" the president demanded.

After Max left the room, the president asked his advisors, "If Chief Seme was a—"

An advisor interrupted, "Sir, I believe it's Keme... Chief Keme."

"Yes...if Chief Keme is a member of the Earth Sentinels, then it makes sense his tribe is as well." The president looked at the foreign relations chairman. "Could you find out if the Canadian prime minister believes the Earth Sentinels are responsible for the recent storms, and if he's willing to stop them?"

"Sir, once we play our hand, it'll eliminate any possibility of covert surveillance," the chairman stated. "We might want to do that first."

"What exactly do you expect to learn through surveillance?" the president asked impatiently. "Couldn't you grab them for interrogation?"

"Mr. President, those people don't live in the US. We'd need the cooperation of the Canadian government."

The president fumed. He didn't like having to ask permission. "So the quandary is…do we do surveillance first, possibly wasting time, or go straight to the top and risk being the laughing stock of Canada for believing in voodoo." The president pondered the predicament a moment. "Let's do the surveillance, but just for a couple days. We don't have time for more. And for Christ's sake, don't get caught!"

Bechard stood next to the crystal ball, watching the president and his staff scheme. He sighed deeply. *Will they never learn?*

CHAPTER 25

Blog Post No. 2

The number of visitors on Norman P. Dunstead's blog had dramatically increased. On one hand, he was happy as a pig in the mud at his blog's newfound popularity, but, on the other hand, he was deeply concerned that the earth was genuinely being invaded by aliens or supernatural forces. The people reading his blog were looking for answers, but he didn't have any. All he could do was write about the events as they happened while hoping he would connect the dots at some point in the near future.

His latest post, "Armageddon is Upon Us," contained a map of the supernatural storms and a pictorial timeline of the previous weather phenomena, starting with the lightning strikes at Bear Claw Lake. He also included a video of Chief Keme being shot, which had been hosted on the Channel 5 News website for a few hours before being replaced by a sanitized version, but not before Norman pirated a copy that he proudly displayed.

CHAPTER 26

Meeting at the Waldorf-Astoria Hotel

After a long day at a UN Security Council meeting, the president and his staff went back to the presidential suite at the historic Waldorf-Astoria Hotel. Longtime White House travel assistant Tyrone Jefferson greeted them at the door, taking their overcoats.

"Pour me a stiff one, would you?" the president asked Tyrone, plopping onto a sofa. "God, I'm so tired. Anyone else like one?"

Tyrone expertly mixed the assorted drinks in crystal glasses, serving them on a silver platter before resuming his post.

As everyone sipped his or her drinks, the president proposed, "What if we didn't fight this? What if we used this opportunity to move forward with alternative fuels?"

One of his advisors said, "Sir, there's nothing wrong with using oil," mostly because he had a cushy job at a big oil company waiting for him after his assignment was over.

The Department of Energy Chief of Staff sighed. "There are much better solutions out there. Let's face it, oil is a dinosaur. No pun intended."

"Without new drilling, fuel prices will sky rocket!" the economic advisor warned.

Another advisor said to the president, "Sir, there are a lot of forces against you on this...big money, namely the fossil fuel boys...the House and Senate, and even the general public doesn't understand the big picture. They just see the price at the pumps.

"And we can't ignore the fact that most people can't afford to pay more for fuel. Some can barely afford food. We'd have to subsidize prices, and we're already trillions in debt."

"Before we go any further," a commanding general interjected, "Have you considered that the Earth Sentinels' power may have peaked? Do we have proof they can carry out their threats?" He sat stiffly on the couch in full uniform waiting for an answer.

The first advisor concurred, "That's a legitimate question. We could ask the Earth Sentinels for proof." Several others nodded in agreement. "But if we ask for a sign, what would it be?"

Denise Zilder, the head at the Environmental Protection Agency, suggested, "How about fixing the water supply in Pennsylvania damaged by fracking?"

The president countered a bit too loudly, "Now, Denise, we don't know for sure that fracking is responsible for those bad wells."

Denise held her tongue, but fumed inside.

The advisor suggested, "How about something sexier, like diffusing the volcano rumbling in Yellow Stone Park? Everyone loves that place!"

The president said, "Yes, but no one knows that's a problem. How about something everyone's familiar with..."

Another advisor spoke up, "How about a flood somewhere? That would make a great visual!"

The president stared at the advisor and thought, *What an idiot.*

The same advisor suggested, "How about a snowstorm in Southern California?"

"Hmmm....that might work," the general agreed.

The president felt they weren't making any traction. "Why don't we meet in the morning after we've had time to think this through?"

CHAPTER 27

The Spy Returns

The psychic searched the spirit realm for two days before rediscovering the Earth Sentinels' domain. Since no one was present, Max took the time to look around, admiring the spiral-patterned stone pavers and ornate benches. He went over to the crystal ball, peering inside, trying to see past the swirling blue mist.

"Looking for something?" Bechard asked, startling Max who jumped back, putting his hands behind his back like a child caught stealing cookies. With a slight quiver in his voice, he answered, "I won't bother explaining. I'm sure you know why I'm here."

Bechard stared at Max. His penetrating eyes and tall stature intimidated the government spy, who felt the fallen angel's energy permeate his soul. "Yes, Max, I know why you are here. It really is pointless to resist our demands, especially when they are for your own good. Why do you fight being helped?"

"I'm not fighting anything. It's just my job."

"Just a job? Saying it's just a job, duty, or whatever you

choose to call it—is just a way of blaming someone else. Ultimately, it is your choice. I believe the Allied Forces prosecuted the World War II German soldiers and officers as war criminals, refusing to accept the excuse, 'I was just following orders.'"

Max was insulted by the analogy and curtly replied, "It's a little harsh comparing me to the Nazis." His righteous indignation faltered. "Anyway, this situation kind of snuck up on me. Usually, I'm searching for the location of an enemy or something like that."

"The enemy? Who is the enemy? Anyone not doing what you want them to do? That doesn't make them wrong."

"How do you know what you're doing is right?" countered Max.

"An excellent question!" Bechard retorted. "The truth is I don't know. There is only one who does and he's not a member of our group."

A chill went down Max's spine.

"Tell me, Max, do you have a problem with our demands?"

"I don't know what your demands are."

"Here, read them, then give me your honest feedback." Bechard handed him a scroll.

As Max read it, he was surprised that the Earth Sentinels had requested nothing for themselves. No riches, positions of power, no country takeovers, just demands that the world use earth-friendly processes.

"You are wrong about that," Bechard explained, "There is something in it for each of us—clean air, clean water, a way of life uninterrupted by people exploiting the earth's resources."

"What's in it for you?" Max asked, perturbed that the angel was reading his mind.

"I prefer to keep the earth around for as long as possible. At this rate, it won't exist much longer, and then what would I do? Go home?" Bechard laughed, flashing his perfect white teeth. "How about you? What's in it for you? A paycheck? A feeling of power? At least be honest with yourself. Tell me, do you care about the earth at all?"

"Of course!"

"Then maybe it's time to prove it," Bechard stated, pausing to let his words sink in. "Join us."

Max was caught off guard by the invitation and hesitated.

Bechard advanced toward Max, who flinched, afraid of retribution, but the fallen angel proceeded past him, waving his hand over the crystal ball. "Look closely," he whispered.

The mist cleared, revealing the earth inside. Max watched the United States come into view, magnifying until the city of New York was clearly visible. Boats moved in and out of the harbor. The spy recognized the Manhattan cityscape. Taxis and cars drove back and forth on the crowded downtown streets. The scene shifted to the UN headquarters lined with world flags, then moved inside to the Security Council chamber. Max saw world leaders and the US president sitting at an enormous round table discussing the crisis created by the Earth Sentinels.

Bechard stared at the glass sphere. "These leaders don't know how to deal with real power. You can let your government use you if you wish, but our cause will succeed." He turned to study Max, who was too scared to look the angel in the eye. "Don't be afraid. I am trying to help you and all of mankind. Again, I ask you...join us. Together, we can make a difference."

Max replied, "I'm sorry, but I can't betray my country."

"But you can betray the world." Bechard sighed. "Very

117

well, tell your president he'll have his sign in the morning. Now leave."

Max left confused. *What sign?* Regardless, he knew he had to relay the message.

CHAPTER 28

The Sign

The US president dreaded getting up the next morning. He lay in the hotel bed wondering what 'sign' was going to happen. *What if it's bad? Will it affect my family?* He cursed himself for being so smug. He looked at the crystal chandelier hanging from the coffered ceiling and the silk draperies that covered the grand windows overlooking Park Avenue, realizing that all the power in the world meant nothing if his family was hurt.

His personal cell phone rang on the nightstand. The caller ID displayed his wife's name. A wave of relief washed over him. He answered it, "Hello!"

"Hello," she responded cheerfully.

"Are you and the kids enjoying Vermont?"

"Yes! It's beautiful this time of year, although a bit chilly, but we're ready to come home."

Still flush with gratitude that his family was safe, he said, "I can't wait to see you and the girls."

She paused. "You seem different. Is everything all right?"

"Lots of pressure here at the UN. God, I'll be so glad when this term is over. I need to spend more time at home."

"Really?" his wife replied, clearly surprised. "The girls would like that."

There was a knock on the hotel door.

"Honey, I've got to go. We'll talk later. I love you." His last three words hung in the air.

"Is everything okay?"

"Yes. Tell the girls I love them."

"Okay, now I'm officially worried."

"Honey, please..."

"Okay, okay, I love you too."

The knock came again.

"Gotta go..."

"Bye."

He put on a bathrobe with the presidential emblem sewn on the breast pocket, then answered the door, but no one was there. Down the hall, four Secret Service body guards stood by the elevator staring straight ahead. They glanced at the president, then resumed their positions.

The president noticed a basket on the floor. It was covered with opalescent cellophane and tied with blue ribbon. *How odd!* he mused, picking it up, reasoning that his assistant must have left it.

Back in the room, he sat on the bed, placing the basket next to himself. He untied the ribbon. The cellophane slid off, revealing a snow globe nestled in blue satin. The president picked it up, peering inside the glass, shocked to see a miniature angel wearing a blue robe and waving at him through the tumbling plastic snow. Afraid, he dropped the snow globe, which bounced on the bedspread.

At this point, a few things ran through the president's mind. *What the hell was that!? Is that a real angel? Is he the Earth Sentinels' leader? Am I losing my mind?*

He hesitantly leaned across the bed to retrieve the snow globe, tilting it upright. The faux snow swirled around the angel, who pointed at the window coverings. The president assumed the angel wanted him to look outside, so he pushed a button on the nightstand. The draperies glided open, but instead of a panoramic view of New York City, the scene was completely white. Confused, the president got up, walking over to the windows. Up close, he noticed snowflakes hitting the glass. A blinding snowstorm raged outside. *Strange for late September,* he thought, checking the snow globe. The angel motioned with his arms, giving a "time out" signal. The blizzard immediately stopped, allowing the president to observe the streets below.

121

The traffic was at a complete standstill. Over a foot of snow had fallen in a matter of minutes. Confused drivers climbed out of their vehicles and pedestrians brushed the snow off their heads and shoulders.

"All right, I believe you!" the president conceded, watching the chaos below. "But I'm not telling anyone about this. They'll have me committed and that idiot vice president will take over." The president looked at the glass ball to see the angel's reaction, but it was empty, except for the snow piled on the bottom.

He tipped the globe upside down, finding the windup key, twisting it several times. The notched cylinder inside moved over thin strips of metal, plucking out the song "Let It Snow". The president smiled as he watched the snow fall inside the globe, partially because he was relieved that nothing too bad had happened, but also because he admired his enemy's clever proof of power. *Maybe the Earth Sentinels will be reasonable after all.*

CHAPTER 29

The Official Response

After three days of emergency meetings at the UN headquarters, the majority of the world's leaders agreed that it wasn't possible to meet the Earth Sentinels' demands in the time frame given. Cost was the main reason cited, but they also felt there weren't enough renewable energy solutions to replace fossil fuels. Countries with nuclear weapon arsenals had no intention of dismantling them, and, last but not least, the leaders refused to submit to an alien force or publicly admit such a force existed.

In an attempt to calm the general public's fears, a UN representative walked into a room filled with members of the media, ready to deliver the official response.

Cameras flashed as the man stepped up to the podium. He slipped on his glasses, reading the prepared statement, "It has been determined by leading scientists that the unnatural thunder storms occurring around the world have been deliberately caused by cloud seeding. For those of you unfamiliar with the term 'cloud seeding', it is when airplanes disperse substances, such as silver iodide, dry ice or salt over clouds with the intention of producing rain.

"This unauthorized manipulation of nature is unacceptable. When the people responsible for these actions are uncovered, they will be severely punished. Thank you." The official pocketed his glasses, then left the room ignoring the reporters' demands for more information.

The President of the United States watched the televised UN press conference from the privacy of his office with two of his most-trusted advisors. When the coverage was over, he shut off the TV.

"Well, sir, that seemed believable," said the first advisor.

"Yes, it did," the other advisor agreed.

The president sat pensively, not saying anything.

"Something wrong, sir?"

"I need to tell you something in the strictest of confidence. Do I have your word you'll tell no one?"

"You have my word, sir." The other advisor agreed as well.

"Two days ago, I received a visit from the Earth Sentinels' leader, the fallen angel Bechard." The president saw the look of disbelief on their faces. "I know it sounds crazy, which is why it needs to remain a secret. But I did see him. You remember the snowstorm in New York?"

"Yes! God, what a mess!"

"That was the angel's doing, proof of their power. The only reason I bring it up is...I'm concerned about the Earth Sentinels' reaction to this announcement. I'd hoped to offer a few concessions, but now, the world would think

I'm nuts blaming the thunderstorms on a fallen angel and spirits. What do you suggest?"

"Well, you could buck the UN and tell Congress, along with the rest of the country, what you just told us. If they believe you and the people don't go hysterical, maybe the lawmakers will put aside their differences and self interests, and work together to implement alternative energy solutions. We could use some of the defense budget to install changes, or restrict people's use of energy—"

The president interrupted, "Okay, okay. I see your point. We'll just wait and see," but privately he thought, *It's gonna have to get worse before it gets better.*

The Prime Minister of the Democratic Republic of the Congo was meeting with the shaman. "Tell me what to do. The UN announced the thunderstorms were an act of cloud seeding, but my people won't believe it. They know witchcraft when they see it."

"Maybe if you switched to earth-friendly methods, our country might be spared," the shaman suggested. "Would the senate and assembly agree to the changes?"

The prime minister contemplated the question, then sighed. "I can't guarantee they'll agree."

"And I can't guarantee the Earth Sentinels will spare our country, but I will ask." The shaman stood up.

The prime minister rose as well. "Let me escort you to the door." He walked with the shaman over the polished mahogany floors. "Please let me know their answer as soon as possible." He opened the front door, noticing his driver outside buffing a black sedan. "I'll have my driver escort you home. It will speed things up." He shouted out the front door, "Manyara! Take this honored guest wherever he needs to go!"

Manyara opened the rear passenger door for the shaman, who got inside the luxurious car, sitting stiffly on the broad leather seat, resting his staff across his lap. He had only ridden in a vehicle a few times in his life, preferring instead to trek across the countryside, letting the dust gather on his feet.

The black sedan left the compound and pulled onto a dirt road. In a few miles, the car was speeding past the grasslands teaming with wildlife.

Suddenly, the situation didn't feel right for the shaman. *What's my hurry?* he thought. *We all reach the same destination in the end. Foolish man, how did you get caught in this web?* "Stop!" he shouted. The driver hit the brakes. "I want out here."

The shaman opened the car door, stepping into the sunlight. He began the long walk toward home, his cane hitting the ground with each stride, humming as the black sedan drove out of sight. A warm breeze caressed his face, causing him to smile. This felt right.

CHAPTER 30

The Second Plan

Thousands of shamans, totem animals and spirits entered the spirit realm, mingling on the courtyard and spilling over the grassy knoll and valley.

Billy moved through the crowd toward Haruto. She was talking with a Tibetan shaman, who was inquiring about the nuclear meltdown in her beloved Japan. Billy tapped her shoulder.

She gracefully spun around. "Why, Mr. White Smoke, how good to see you!" The dragon dutifully positioned next to her scowled at him.

Billy ignored the reptilian sentinel, instead focusing on Haruto's dark-brown eyes. "It's good to see you!" His voice was a tad too high. He cleared his throat, finding his usual deep tone to compliment her, "You look beautiful as always." *Did I just say that?* he agonized internally, embarrassed.

The dragon snorted patronizingly, billowing smoke out of his snout. Haruto and Billy coughed, waving their hands to clear the air.

Cheva followed Zachary as he searched for Conchita. The massive horse moved like a bull in a china shop, knocking and bumping into people as he made his way through the tightly knit group, continually apologizing, "So sorry. Excuse me. Sorry..."

The fallen angel soared across the sky, capturing the attention of the members who hushed. His impressive wings flapped as he descended, casting a breeze over the crowd. He gently landed, tucking his wings and raising his arms. Bechard thundered, "Welcome, Earth Sentinels!" The ocean floated in his blue eyes and the universe danced in his raven black hair. He lowered his arms, examining those standing before him. "It appears we have work to do. The world has refused our demands, forcing us to increase our display of power. An unfortunate necessity, I'm afraid." He let his words sink in. "There are many injustices on Earth. That's why you're here. So now, we must decide how to proceed. Ideas anyone?"

Nobody spoke up.

Bechard said, "I realize coming up with a solution is difficult. Why don't we remind ourselves what we are fighting against?" He swept his hand over the crystal ball. The blue mist dissolved, displaying the nuclear meltdown in Fukushima, Japan, for a moment, then the earth spun again. When it stopped, it showed the abandoned cities surrounding Chernobyl—ghostly reminders of a radioactive disaster decades earlier. Spinning again, the earth unveiled current oil spills, one after another. Then images of barren land appeared where rainforests used to stand. Rows of windowless barns came into view. Inside each building were stacks of small cages, row upon row, containing sickly chickens with missing feathers, unable to stand or turn around. Deserted communities were

128

shown where the fracking process had ruined the water supply and dispersed toxic chemicals into the air.

Sensing the Earth Sentinels had seen enough, Bechard waved his hand over the crystal ball. The images ceased. He waited until everyone settled down, then said, "Would the totem animals come forward, please?"

Cheva, Kane, Taslia, the dragon and hundreds of other totem animals slithered, swam, flew and stepped forward. Bechard said to them, "I have an idea, but need your help." The totem animals were curious. "I am recommending that, for one day only, the creatures of Earth attack mankind. Excluding the children, of course."

The totem animals were speechless.

Haruto gave her opinion first, "I don't think we want to become cold-hearted killers. You say spare the children, but who will take care of the children if their parents are dead?"

"What if the world retaliates and starts killing the animals? It will be a blood bath. No one would win," stated Billy.

"How about a 'natural' disaster instead? Giant earthquakes and tsunamis," suggested a shaman.

Someone shouted, "That would also kill the animals!"

Pahtia asked, "What is a tsunami?"

"Let me show you," Bechard offered. A holographic projection appeared over the glass ball, showing a thousand-foot wave swelling over a city. Haruto looked away, reminded of the disaster her city had recently endured. The image abruptly vanished, but the devastation potential was clearly understood.

A shaman from India asked, "What if we live near the coast? I don't want to plan the death of my own people."

129

Zachary lamented, "I can't do this! I can't kill people!" He still felt immense guilt about the oil rigger who had died and couldn't imagine how he would feel killing thousands, or even millions, of people.

Bechard motioned for everyone to calm down. "If we don't intercede, mankind will self destruct. All of it... including you and your family. I know this seems severe, but humanity is oblivious to subtle messages."

"What if we give them a blueprint to follow? Show them how to create alternative energy solutions?" suggested a shaman from China.

Bechard answered, "We have repeatedly inspired your best scientists, engineers and even lay people, who developed renewable fuel options. However, time after time, their patents were bought under false pretenses and shelved by fossil fuel companies wanting to squash the competition, and when the inventors refused to sell, they were often killed. Until the resistance is eliminated, it's an endless battle. By the time the world is willing to use alternative energy, it will be too late."

The shaman from the Congo Republic asked, "If my country cooperates, can we be spared?"

A German shaman spoke up, "Germany is already fast tracking alternative energy and will eliminate all nuclear plants within ten years! We want protection from the attacks!"

Looking around the crowd, Bechard inquired, "Should countries implementing alternative energy methods be spared? Or will our message become diluted if it is not applied worldwide? For instance, the supernatural storms over the capitols of the world would have been ignored if they had appeared random. And although the world

130

resisted our demands, we did instigate an emergency UN meeting. The greatest powers on Earth were afraid!"

Billy asked, "If we ask the animals to kill people, what kind of message will that send?"

"Excellent question," Bechard said. "Why don't we address the pros and cons..."

A shaman shouted, "It'll remind people they're not in control!"

Bechard flicked his hand. The words "Not in control" materialized out of thin air. The blue misty letters floated over the crowd.

Another shaman yelled, "It'll show we're fighting back! Enough is enough!"

The words "Enough is enough" hovered near the previous words.

A Greenland shaman called out, "People might become afraid and retaliate."

The word "Retaliation" appeared.

"Will it make us cold-hearted killers?" a Brazilian shaman wondered out loud.

The words "Cold-hearted killers" became visible.

Zachary asked, "What about the animals? After they've attacked, how will it affect them? Will they feel ashamed? Will they continue to kill?"

The words "After effects" arose, then all of the words spun, intermingling before disappearing in a puff of smoke.

"Why don't we ask the totem animals for their perspectives?" Bechard suggested.

Cheva spoke first, "I understand the cycle of life on Earth, but animals do not kill out of hatred or maliciousness, unless they are sick. We would be asking creatures to go against their—"

Billy interrupted, directing his question to Bechard, "Who would you attack? What justifies one person becoming a victim while another lives? Who's to say it wouldn't be you or me? Why don't we stick with isolated storms that disrupt governments and business? We can close down highways, airports, businesses. If they can't make money, they'll listen."

"Do you really think so?" Chief Keme asked. "We've been negotiating for centuries. The government doesn't keep its word. They steal our land and children, kill us..." He unconsciously placed his hand on his heart.

"If we attack, the world will hate us and go to the ends of the earth to find us," warned the old Siberian shamaness. "Why do you think I live in the wilderness where no one wants to go? People are afraid of my power." The owl on her shoulder hooted softly. She absentmindedly stroked his chest with her calloused hand. "I have never purposely hurt anyone, but then who knows what is right or wrong? I have to trust the spirits' guidance for that, and I don't see any divine beings in our group. Perhaps that should tell us something." She stared at Bechard, thinking it had been a mistake dealing with the fallen angel.

"All of us are imperfect or we wouldn't be here," Bechard replied. "Each of you received guidance from your spirit guides and weren't happy with it, which is why you joined the Earth Sentinels. However, you are free to leave at anytime. But if you do, remember it is extremely important to keep your identities secret, otherwise, the governments will use you to get at the others."

Billy suggested, "We should give this more thought. It's too important to rush in to."

"Yes, it is important," Bechard acknowledged. "How

about we reconvene in three days' time? Give everyone a chance to think it over. Sound good?"

Everyone agreed, solemnly dispersing through the invisible doorways between the spirit realm and Earth. Chief Keme waved goodbye to his tribe members.

Zachary struggled through the crowd trying to get to Conchita, who was being led away by Pahtia. "Wait!" he shouted, but it was too late.

She and her father stepped through the doorway.

133

Chapter 31

Second Guessing

On a dreary morning, Billy pulled his old truck into the driveway at Zachary's house. The tires crunched over the limestone. He shut off the ignition, but the engine continued to sputter and cough before finally shuddering to a standstill. He opened the creaky door and got out, patting the hood as he walked by. *You're an embarrassment, old girl.*

Billy stepped onto the porch, knocking on the front door. The dogs ran over to greet him.

Larry answered, "Hello? Ah, it's you again. Come on in." He shooed the dogs away. "I'll let Zachary know you're here." Billy stood in the entryway while Larry called up the stairs, "Zach! Your friend's here!"

"Be right down!"

Larry and Billy awkwardly waited. To pass the time, Larry asked, "So, what do you two have planned?"

"Walk in the woods. Connect with nature."

Larry nodded, unsure if he believed the man.

Zachary ambled down the stairs. "Hello, Billy! Want something to drink? We got bottled water, juice."

"No thanks. Had coffee on the way over."

Larry interjected, "I want to show you two something," surprising both Billy and Zachary who followed him into the garage where he flipped on a fluorescent light. Inside was a giant, plastic container full of water. "Just delivered today. They call it a water buffalo." Larry laughed bitterly. "Now we can take showers! One of life's little perks." Larry paused. His face grew glum. "Look, I'd love to blow those companies off the face of the earth, literally," he growled. "The laws protect them, but nobody's protecting us." He looked at his son, "But be careful. I don't want to lose you over this."

Larry fed the dogs behind the house while Zachary and Billy walked across the backyard, heading toward the woods. The milk cow mooed as they passed the barn.

The men trudged along the tractor path next to the field littered with withered crop stalks. The harvest was over and no one knew if there would be another one.

"They've started rebuilding the fracking rigs," Zachary bitterly complained. "Putting bigger lightning rods at the top, like that's going to help." Billy remained silent, letting him vent. "I don't want to hurt anyone, but when I see all the devastation, it makes me so mad and depressed, I can barely get out of bed. Nobody seems to care!"

They found the deer path that led into the woods and followed it. Fallen leaves crunched beneath their feet. A squirrel scampered up a tree. A family of crows cawed in the branches of an old oak tree before taking to flight, turning into silhouettes against the gray sky.

When the men came to the tree that had cried for help, Billy reached in his back pocket, taking out a pouch

135

of tobacco. He offered it to Zachary, who took a pinch, sprinkling it at the base of the tree, saying, "We honor you. May we sit in your branches?"

The wind picked up. Leaves tumbled across the forest floor and over his shoes. The tree swayed, dancing in the wind. A woodsy breath whirled around the young man's face, weakly whispering, "Sit with me."

Zachary climbed into her branches.

Billy followed him.

After they were settled, Zachary mentioned, "It feels right defending the earth, at least in principle, but I'm afraid if we start killing, it won't feel right. You know?"

"I know."

"What are you gonna do?"

"Don't let me influence you. I know it's scary making your own decisions, but I wouldn't be doing you any favors making it for you. Best I can say is, 'Follow your heart.'" Then without saying another word, Billy climbed down and walked away.

Zachary was left alone to make the most important decision of his young life.

Chapter 32

Spying on the Bear Claw Tribe

On a hill overlooking the Bear Claw First Nation reservation, two CIA agents stood next to a telephone pole pretending to be utility workers. Two more agents sat in the van listening to snippets of private conversations. "...I'll be back by nine..." "Hey...your father home?" After a few hours of mind-numbing boredom, the agents heard what sounded like a pertinent conversation, "...after what they did to Chief Keme, they deserve it. I don't have any problem going through with it."

"Shhhh...someone will hear you."

"I don't care, they can rot in hell!"

One agent said to the other, "Sounds like they're plotting something."

"They're always plotting something."

In the spirit realm, Bechard peered into the crystal ball watching the CIA agents. *Spying on my fellow Earth Sentinels are you? I'll have to put an end to that.* He touched the glass with his fingers, sending two lightning bolts coursing through the atmosphere toward the eavesdroppers.

One bolt hit the telephone pole, covering it with electric fingers that sizzled toward the ground, engulfing the agents standing nearby. Both men convulsed as the electricity clawed through their bodies. The other bolt struck the van, causing it to explode.

Bechard dusted his hands together, admiring the charred remains. *Well, that ought to buy some time.*

The explosion echoed throughout the valley. The Bear Claw Tribe members hurried out of their houses to see what had happened. Cecile and Tom observed the black smoke at the top of the hill.

"Wonder who screwed up this time?" Cecile asked.

Tom answered, "It's either the oil company or government. Nobody else is that stupid."

Later that evening, Tom flipped on the Channel 5 News and saw Lisa Bantoné broadcasting live at the scene.

She reported, "The Canadian government gave an official statement late this afternoon." She looked at a piece of paper in her hand. "And I quote, 'The explosion near Bear Claw Lake has taken the lives of four dedicated public service employees. Right now, we do not know if it was in retaliation to the recent killing of Chief Keme, who was shot by the Royal Canadian Army. We will investigate this matter thoroughly. However, as of today, no arrests have been made.' End quote." The camera panned to show the torched van and utility pole. The area was roped off with yellow police tape. Lisa narrated, "There's speculation that the Bear Claw Tribe members who have been aggressively protesting the oil spill at the nearby lake may have done this...upset over the death of Chief Keme, who as I mentioned a moment ago, was shot by the Canadian Army. I want to emphasize that no one knows for sure who is behind this attack. Back to you, Gary."

The anchorman responded, "Lisa, our thoughts and prayers go out to the victims' families."

An enraged Tom ran out of his house, down the dirt lane to Cecile's place. He banged on the door, yelling, "Cecile! Cecile!"

She opened the door, rubbing her sleepy eyes, "What, Neechie?" He pushed his way inside. Empty beer cans were scattered over the coffee table.

"Did you see the news?" Cecile shook her head, afraid of what Tom was about to tell her. "They framed us for the explosion!" She groggily stared at him, not comprehending what he was trying to say. Tom clarified, "Four men died up there!"

Cecile's mind became alert as the adrenaline kicked in. "What!? No! We never win. When we stand our ground, we're killed, and when we do nothing, we're framed!"

Tom tilted his head back, facing heaven, sighing heavily. "Great Spirit, why must we suffer for so long?"

Cecile suddenly grabbed his arm, startling him. "They know! The government knows!"

"That we're Earth Sentinels?"

She nodded, then cried out, "Why did we think we could win!? They'll kill us, just like they always do!" She collapsed onto the green, tattered chair in her living room, resting her head in her hands, feeling overwhelmed. Light filtered through the metal blinds hanging in the front window.

Tom reached over, stroking the top of her head to

soothe her. "If we are to die, then let us die as warriors. I'm tired of being powerless."

Cecile raised her head. "I'm gonna tell Bechard I'm on board."

"Me, too. If the world won't protect us, we'll protect ourselves."

CHAPTER 33

The New Plan

The Earth Sentinels regrouped three days later hoping to finalize a new plan. As soon as Zachary arrived, he searched the crowd. Conchita smiled broadly when she saw his handsome face coming her way until her father stepped between them, intercepting the young man. "Can I help you?"

"Sir, I'd like to speak with your daughter."

The shaman sighed, contemplating how to get rid of him, but at that moment, another Amazonian shaman approached Pahtia to introduce himself.

Zachary used this window of opportunity to sneak past Conchita's father and greet her, "It's nice to meet you, I'm Zachary..."

She grabbed his arm, whisking him away, far from her father. They zigzagged through the people, then stood behind an ancient tree at the edge of the courtyard.

She began assailing Zachary with questions, "Are you a shaman?"

"I just learned how...my friend Billy taught me."

"Is he a shaman?"

"I don't think so...I think he just practices the old ways. Not sure he has a tribe."

"Do you have a tribe?"

He smiled knowing she was isolated from the rest of the world. "No, our society doesn't have tribes. We barely have families."

"You can be a part of my tribe. An honorary member!" She laughed. Zachary loved the way she expressed herself without restraint. He also admired her exotic features.

Conchita tugged at his shirt. "You wear too many clothes! What are you hiding?"

He thought, *I'd love to show you what I'm hiding*, but then felt guilty when she smiled innocently at him.

"CONCHITA!" her father shouted, startling both of them. Pahtia grabbed his daughter's arm, dragging her away.

Zachary was broken hearted watching Conchita go.

Billy came up behind him and said, "Love is fraught with perils."

"I don't know what that means," Zachary responded, losing sight of her.

"Nobody said it was going to be easy, kid."

"Really? How's it going with you and Haruto?"

"Couldn't be better," Billy gloated, but his smile faded when a puff of smoke drifted past him. He turned to face Haruto. The dragon standing next to her snorted, sending another plume of smoke his way.

"Hello, Mr. White Cloud," Haruto said curtly.

"Umm...it's White Smoke," Billy corrected her.

She forced a smile. "My mistake. I believe you were talking about me. Would you care to repeat it?"

Billy could only see one way out of this mess. He complimented her, "Have I ever told you how beautiful you are?"

"Yes."

"Smart, wise, loving?" Billy added sheepishly.

Haruto stared emotionlessly at him.

"Irresistible, powerful, and excellent taste in men," Billy continued, a bit more boldly.

She tried, but couldn't prevent a slight smile appearing on her face. Billy grinned, melting her heart.

Bechard captured their attention by calling out, "Welcome, Earth Sentinels! It is time to begin!" The fallen angel waited for everyone to take their places. Zachary and Billy sat on a stone bench beside Haruto. There wasn't room for the dragon pouting behind them. "Thanks for coming. It appears a few members have left our group," Bechard commented, glancing around. "But we'll respect their decision and move forward. I know you've given this a lot of thought and I encourage you to share your ideas."

Zachary was uneasy at being the first, but felt confident about his solution. He stood up. Bechard nodded, encouraging him to begin. Clearing his throat, Zachary offered his opinion, "I believe Billy mentioned this last time, and I agree. We could use storms to strategically disrupt the world. Have them hit major cities, airports, stadiums—just long enough to upset people and gain their attention."

"It's not big enough!" someone shouted.

The others grumbled similar thoughts.

Bechard held up his hand to silence them. "This has more potential than you realize. First, it would gain the public's attention, who frankly have been going on with their daily lives through all of this, and nobody cares until it impacts them. It's sure to attract the media, which means the government will have to respond. It's a fairly compassionate solution that will scare the bejeebers out of everyone!"

Chief Keme spoke up, "I think we need to add something to this. Something that will prevent governments from stating it's a natural or manmade occurrence."

"I have an idea," Bechard said with a gleam in his eye.

CHAPTER 34

The Supernatural Storms

Norman P. Dunstead had taken a break from writing his blog to watch a televised Chicago Bears game. He jumped up cheering as the quarterback ran into the end zone, but his enthusiasm waned when a flag was thrown. He sank onto the sofa hoping the penalty was against the other team.

The announcer said, "Only twenty-seconds until halftime. It will definitely change the scope of this game if the Bears get to keep this touchdown."

The camera panned away from the referees conferencing on the field, past the anxious spectators, focusing on the sky over the stadium where a black storm cloud in the shape of a bear lumbered over the arena. Music blared and the fans cheered, celebrating the awesome sight. The announcer exclaimed, "Wow! Looks like our boys got a little ahead of themselves. That's some cool animation!"

The other announcer agreed, "Yes, incredible! Must be for the halftime show. Is that a hologram?" He shuffled through his papers looking for any mention of a 3D display on the schedule.

The crowd rallied.

A group of shirtless men danced, showing off their flabby chests and beer bellies painted orange and blue.

The referees stopped talking and the players forgot about the game as they watched the bear-shaped storm drift over the 50-yard line where it opened its mouth, shooting a bolt of lightning at a goal post.

Sparks flew.

The fans stopped cheering. Everyone became confused.

Smoke rose from the blackened metal.

The announcer yelled, "What was that!?"

The bear-shaped storm rumbled. Its mouth opened again, spewing lightning at a cluster of stadium lights that exploded. A section of the stands went dark. Screams filled the arena.

Norman stared at the screen that showed the storm moving away from the athletic field, disappearing into the night sky. He scratched his head, wondering if the bear-shaped storm had been overly realistic halftime entertainment.

The wind picked up outside Norman's apartment. He got off the sofa to peek outside, stunned to see the same bear-shaped storm towering over the Chicago skyline.

"Holy shit! Holy shit!" he yelled, running into the kitchen to grab his phone off the counter, dashing back to the window.

Just as he began recording, the bear-shaped storm turned its head, seeming to stare directly at Norman with its fiery eyes. The blogger's heart skipped a beat. Adrenaline coursed through his body as the storm marched closer, encompassing his building.

Lightning flashed in every direction.

The building shook, windows rattled, and the lights and TV flickered off, leaving Norman standing in the dark.

Then the storm passed.

Shaking with excitement, Norman replayed the video on his phone. The city lights illuminated the storm's distinct grizzly figure. *This is so awesome!* he thought.

The Manhattan skyscrapers towered over the evening traffic below. A sudden gust of wind threw open the pedestrians' coats. Trash blew in the air and street signs shook.

The people looked up and saw a horse-shaped storm cloud looming over the tall buildings. Lightning flared down its cumulus legs and hooves. Its red, glowing eyes examined the people cowering on the sidewalks below. The feral storm snorted and shook its head, sending streaks of electricity bursting from its mane.

The pedestrians ran screaming in terror as the storm galloped through the air, breaking windows and crumpling awnings.

Cars were blown out of their lanes, hitting other vehicles, bringing traffic to a halt.

The horse-shaped storm bolted down the midway, heading toward LaGuardia Airport.

The Bear Claw Tribe gathered around a campfire roasting a pig and drinking a keg of beer. Their celebration had two purposes. The first was to raise the tribe's spirits, which were extremely low after Chief Keme's death, and the other was to celebrate the supernatural storms currently besieging the world. The tribe hoped their prayers would be answered after tonight.

"Look! There it is!" a man exclaimed.

Everyone saw the stag-shaped storm cloud thundering across the sky. The weather phenomenon bowed its head acknowledging the tribe members below. Its massive set of antlers mingled with the twinkling stars.

On the other side of the world, an owl-shaped storm glided across the morning sky in Moscow. Lightning surged inside the turbulent cloud formation, frightening everyone on the streets below.

The people fled into houses and shops to escape the fire bolts. Safely inside, they pressed their noses against the windows, watching the eerie storm pass over.

CHAPTER 35

The President's Reaction

The morning after the supernatural storms struck, it wasn't surprising that the first thing the US president did was call an emergency meeting with his advisors. The American people were terrified, fearing an alien invasion, or worse, the wrath of God.

"Well, gentlemen, I'd like to discuss our strategy for dealing with the supernatural storms obviously caused by the Earth Sentinels," the president stated. "What do we tell the public?"

A commanding general addressed the group, "We could say that the indigenous people used black magic to conjure these storms. And since the Canadian tribe is part of the Earth Sentinels, it's safe to assume the US tribes are as well." The general looked around the room reading everyone's faces. They seemed receptive, so he continued, "Making indigenous people the number one enemy of this country would allow us to round them up as domestic terrorists. They're most likely guilty anyway, so it's not like we're doing anything wrong."

One of the advisors interjected, "We don't know for sure that the US tribes are part of the Earth Sentinels, although I believe they are. But if we rush in there without public support, we'll have a PR nightmare on top of the problems we've already got. This is a unique situation, because technically, they're American citizens. We need to show good faith. Maybe invite them to the White House for a powwow." The men chuckled at the inappropriate remark.

"They've got a tribal council," the general mentioned. "If we could get the chiefs in here, we could arrest 'em. Say that they tried to attack the president or something."

"What if they counter attack?" asked another advisor. "The Earth Sentinels have shown some extreme powers!"

"Yes, but the Earth Sentinels can't possibly protect all the tribes at the same time. We could invade the reservations simultaneously. Great chance to try out our new drones and armored vehicles!" the general pointed out.

The advisor persisted, "What about the list of demands? What if that information leaks out? Everyone will know the tribes weren't trying to take over the world, and we'll look like assholes beating up the little guys."

The general didn't give a damn about public opinion. "We'll say the list is fake, claim it's a conspiracy theory, a forged document. We'll tell everyone the tribes threatened us because they want their land back. The public will believe us. They always do. And once the people fear them, they'll demand we kill them."

The president was a little put off by the general's enthusiasm for killing people, but reasoned, *If the military did get rid of the tribes, it would open up a lot of natural resources at no cost.* And that would make his friends at the mining and lumber companies very happy. But the president worried that the Earth Sentinels might attack him personally. *All the more reason to quickly get rid of them,* he rationalized, then announced, "I'm ready to move forward. Create a plan and present it to me this afternoon. I'll talk with other leaders to get them on board."

151

CHAPTER 36

The Empire Strikes Back

Zachary had been glued to the TV news coverage of the supernatural storms all morning as he anxiously waited for the government's response. A message flashed on the screen alerting viewers that the President of the United States was about to hold a press conference. Zachary sat upright.

The president stepped up to the podium. "Hello, fellow Americans! This morning, thousands of people are still without electricity because of the strange storms that occurred last night. While an inconvenience, it should only take a few days to get affected areas back up and running. A special thanks to our dedicated public utilities employees working around the clock to get the job done."

As the president took a breath, the reporters shouted questions.

One yelled, "Who's behind these storms?"

"Aliens?" another reporter called out. "Have they made contact?"

The president held up his hand to quiet the journalists.

"The supernatural storms were acts of geo-terrorism."

The reporters gasped, looking at each other, trying to determine if they had heard the president correctly.

"Never in the history of this great country has a leader dealt with attacks of this nature. Our intelligence agencies are working hard to gather all the facts, but preliminary information indicates that the indigenous people, here and abroad, worked with unseen forces to create the unnatural storms we saw last night. This group refers to itself as the Earth Sentinels, and they are demanding control of the world. Should our initial intelligence prove true, we'll do whatever it takes to defend our great nation against these terrorist acts."

The reporters went nuts.

"Every tribe in the world!?" a journalist cried out in disbelief.

"What proof do you have that Native Americans created these storms?" yelled another.

Zachary stared at the TV in disbelief as the president answered the reporters, repeatedly demonizing the tribes. Zachary tightened his lips, trying not to cry, but then a defiant look came over his face.

He ran upstairs to his room where he uploaded the photo of the scroll from his phone to his computer.

Zachary pulled into the parking lot of the two-story office building surrounded by fenced satellite dishes. A large, lit sign read, "Channel 12 News." He gathered his courage as he walked across the parking lot, hesitating a moment before opening the glass door.

At the front desk, he asked to speak with a reporter. A minute later, a man wearing a tie greeted him in the

153

lobby, shaking his hand, "Nice to meet you. You said you had information regarding the supernatural storms?" Zachary nodded. "Come with me." The reporter led him to a cubicle, giving him the sole chair. "Please have a seat. Tell me what you know." The reporter remained standing, leaning against his desk.

Zachary uncomfortably explained why the Earth Sentinels created the supernatural storms, then handed the man an envelope.

The reporter pulled out a piece of paper. "What's this?"

"It's a copy of the scroll that was delivered to the president. It lists the Earth Sentinels' demands. All the world leaders received one."

At this point, the reporter became even more skeptical, but he read the scroll's message to humor Zachary. "This is very interesting, but how do I know you didn't write this yourself? I can't go on air with an unverified document. I'll look like an idiot."

"Funny, no one asks the government to verify their sources and you know they're liars."

The reporter laughed, nodding his head in agreement.

Zachary continued, "Our country is about to attack all the indigenous tribes, although only a few are actually involved. You can see there are no demands for money or power, only that everyone treat the earth with respect."

The reporter countered, "There're a couple of problems. First, no government has admitted the scroll exists, and second, you're just a kid. That takes your credibility down a notch or two. At face value, I believe you, but the director will never let me broadcast this. Unless...could you provide the name of someone to corroborate your story."

"I can't do that. There must be another way."

"You could give me a heads up before the next event."

"It'll be too late! They'll all be dead! Forget it! I'm going to another station," Zachary threatened.

"Tell you what. I'll run it by my—"

Frustrated, Zachary interrupted him, "Do your best, I gotta go," then rushed out of the cubicle.

Zachary drove home wiping tears from his eyes. *This is all my fault. I've got to do something!* He pulled into the driveway, hurrying inside the house.

His parents were watching the television in the living room and didn't notice him rushing up the stairs to his room where he got on the computer, searching the Internet for conspiracy bloggers. At the top of the results was a blog titled "Earth Sentinels Strike Again" by Norman P. Dunstead, featuring the Bear Claw Lake oil spill, lightning strikes, the death of Chief Keme, and the recent animal-shaped storms. Zachary sent Norman an email that explained the Earth Sentinels' goals and actions, and included a photo of the scroll, then he browsed for other bloggers who might be interested in the story.

Ding! An email alert sounded. Norman wrote that he was very interested and would write the post immediately.

Wearing a winter coat, a very excited Norman sat in his cold apartment. With anticipation, he rubbed his hands together trying to warm them. He picked up his phone and began typing with his thumbs.

A low battery warning flashed on the screen.

Shit! It's always something, he thought, but then

calmed himself. Norman wasn't going to let this minor setback dampen his good spirits. After all, he gleefully mused, *When this post is finished, it will make world news! Maybe even WikiLeaks! But first, let's get this baby charged.*

The hum of the Windy City was heard in the distance as Norman walked on the sidewalk past his apartment complex to the nearby bus stop. He waited next to an old lady, a mother and her two small children, and an unkempt man.

Suddenly three black sedans with dark-tinted windows sped down the street. The cars screeched to a halt, double parking next to the curb. Men dressed identically in black suits and dark reflective sunglasses spilled out of the vehicles, running inside Norman's apartment building.

The blogger wondered what was going on, but his thoughts were interrupted by the arrival of the bus. Its air brakes hissed and doors opened. While Norman waited for the others to board, he looked up at his apartment window and saw one of the men wearing dark sunglasses walk past. Dumbfounded, Norman stepped onboard and found an empty seat where he contemplated what had just happened. *Shit!* the blogger thought, *The government knows!*

He quickly pulled out his phone, using its precious battery reserves to warn Zachary that government agents were heading his way. Then it occurred to Norman that the FBI, CIA, NSA, or whoever the hell it was in the black sedans, could trace him by the GPS in his phone, prompting him to remove the battery. Initially, he felt better, but quickly became nervous again, thinking it was too little, too late.

He got off at the next stop, leaving his phone on the seat, walking several blocks to a busier street where he hailed a cab.

The cabbie was an immigrant from India. His vehicle was well maintained and featured a statue of Buddha on the dashboard. The driver started the meter, then hit the gas, throwing Norman against the seat. "Where to?"

"Umm…" Norman had no idea where he wanted to go. His only concern at the moment was distancing himself from the government agents.

The driver made conversation, "Did you lose electricity?"

"Yes. My apartment's freezing and I need a place to stay." This was only partially true. Norman didn't believe he'd ever be able to return. "I'd like to stop at my bank."

"Sure. Which one?" The cabbie stopped at the intersection. The streetlight was out, so he checked both ways before proceeding.

"Chicago Trust."

"There is one in Cicero. It's good there. Okay?"

"Yes, that's fine." Norman reasoned he could use the time to decide where to go next.

The cabbie interrupted his thoughts, "I have an empty place. It was my mother-in-law's, bless her. You could rent it. It has a private entrance and cheaper than a hotel, if you can find one."

Norman liked this suggestion. The place would be "off the grid" and untraceable by the government—if he paid by cash. "That might work. Where do you live?"

"Berwyn."

Great! thought Norman. *It's not too close to where I*

157

live. "When can I see it?"

"As soon as you go to bank, we go right after. I own my own taxi...make my own hours!" the cabbie exclaimed, turning on the satellite radio to play music from the '80s.

When the driver reached the bank, he double parked out front, ignoring the honking car behind them.

"Can you wait here?" Norman asked.

"Sure! If traffic cop comes, I will go around the block," he made a circle with his finger, "Don't worry, I will be here. Okay?"

"Yeah, sure. I won't be long."

Norman went through the revolving door, approaching the counter. Bulletproof glass separated him and the bank teller, who spoke through a microphone, "How can I help you?"

"I'd like to empty my account."

"I'll need your driver's license, account number and password," she requested nonchalantly.

He slid the ID and info under the glass.

The teller pulled up his account. "Would you like this as a cashier's check or transferred to another account?"

"No, I'd like cash, please."

"Just a moment. I'll need the manager's approval."

After what seemed like an eternity, the woman returned to tell him, "We can only give you five thousand today. You'll need to schedule an appointment for larger amounts."

Norman fumed inside. *It's my money! I didn't have to make an appointment to deposit it!* But he hid his irritation, asking, "Could you make an exception? Perhaps seventy-five hundred?"

"I'm sorry, but everyone's coming in because of the

storm needing cash. We have to serve everyone."

Reasoning that it was unlikely he'd be able to access his account again, he decided to take what he could. "I'd like it all in twenties."

After the teller put the bundles of bills in several envelopes, she pushed it through the security slot. Norman stuffed the money in his pockets and wallet, walking out of the bank feeling extremely vulnerable.

The taxi was waiting by the entrance.

Norman jumped in.

The driver put his hand on the shifter, looked in the rearview mirror and asked, "Where to, friend?"

"The closest business center. I need to use a computer." Norman nervously glanced out the window. "Hurry, please!"

In a few blocks, they found one located in the lower level of a building, the sign barely visible above the cars parked on the street.

159

"I shouldn't be more than twenty minutes," Norman said, opening the door.

The cabbie tapped the meter. He had no intention of being left with a large tab. Norman took a few bills out of his wallet, and then stepped onto the sidewalk, heading down the stairs.

The blogger opened the glass door and looked around the premises. Every computer was occupied except for one in the farthest corner. Norman quickly scooted across the room. He sat down, but didn't touch the computer immediately. He was worried that as soon as he logged into his blog or email account the government would pinpoint his location. He went through the steps in his mind, *First, I'll write the copy in a word program, paste it into my blog, and then get the photo from my email account. That should give me a few minutes before the agents storm this place. Yes, that'll work! If nothing goes wrong.*

Norman anxiously wrote the article, divulging the Earth Sentinels' quest to save the planet. After quickly proofing it, he logged into his blog feeling like a sitting duck. Perspiration beaded on his forehead as he pasted in the copy. Next, he downloaded the photo of the scroll from his email account, and then uploaded it to the blog.

He moved the cursor over the "publish" button, but hesitated to click it, wondering if he was part of a giant hoax. His finger remained poised over the mouse as he contemplated how all those years of building up his blog's reputation would go down the drain if he was wrong. Then he felt an odd pressure on his finger, as if someone was pressing on it, causing him to click the mouse.

The post published.

Too late now, he thought, jumping up, racing out of the business center, dropping a 20-dollar bill on the sales counter as he sped by.

Norman rushed up the stairs to the street level. On the sidewalk, he twisted his head back and forth looking for his taxi. It wasn't there. He briskly rounded the corner, sighing with relief at the sight of the familiar cab idling by the curb.

He climbed in, collapsing against the black vinyl seat.

The taxi pulled away, blending into the traffic.

Behind them, a black sedan screeched to a halt in front of the business center.

160

CHAPTER 37

Hiding Out

After the blogger had contacted him, Zachary grabbed his jacket, rushing down the stairs, snagging the keys by the door.

His mother called out, "Are you leaving!?"

But he was already gone.

Zachary put the farm truck in gear, racing out of the driveway, peeling the tires when he hit the pavement. *Shit! How could I be so stupid?*

Driving the truck as fast as he could over the bumpy trail that ran through the trees, Zachary saw the silver bullet trailer come into view. He jerked to a stop behind Billy's old pickup, hurrying out, pounding on the front door. From inside, the hound dog bayed, making the young man feel like an intruder.

"Hey!" Billy shouted from behind him.

Alarmed, Zachary spun around. "Damnit! Stop sneaking up on me!"

Billy laughed. "But it's so easy to do!"

Zachary's face remained sullen. "I'm in trouble."

Billy's smiled vanished. "Come inside. Let's talk."

When the door opened, the dog shut up.

Zachary looked around the trailer. It was tidier than he had expected for a bachelor. The tiny kitchen abutted an even tinier living room, which consisted of a built-in "sofa" and a small television resting on a hinged tray attached to the wall.

Buddy came out from under the sofa, sheepishly wagging his tail.

"It's okay." Billy petted the dog on the head, then said to Zachary, "Have a seat. Tell me what's wrong."

Too upset to sit, Zachary blurted, "They've found me!"

Billy rubbed his chin, giving this some thought. "Where's your phone?"

Zachary patted his jacket and pant pockets. "Hmmm, not sure I brought it. Maybe it's in the truck."

"Go check. If it is, we need to get out of here."

Zachary had a blank look on his face.

Billy explained, "Phones have GPS—"

"Oh, shit!"

He hurried outside. Billy and Buddy followed him.

Zachary frantically searched the driver's side while Billy checked the passenger seat and floor.

After a few minutes, Zachary conceded, "I must have left it in my room," closing the rusty door.

Buddy sniffed a tire, lifting his leg to pee on it.

"That's a lucky break," Billy stated. "Tell me, how'd they found out?"

"They traced an email I sent to a blogger." He justified his actions, "Did you hear the government's announcement this morning!? They're plotting a war against the indigenous tribes, lumping them all together as Earth Sentinels!"

"No, I didn't hear, but nothing the government does surprises me anymore."

"Yeah, well, I found this blogger who's been following us, so he seemed like a good fit. I thought if more people knew about the scroll and the *real* demands, maybe it would prevent the attack on the tribes. I guess I should've waited instead of going off on my own." Zachary grimaced. "One more thing, I emailed fifty news stations and delivered one in person."

Billy lifted his hat and smoothed his hair back, letting out a long sigh. "Well, kid, gotta admit when you do something, you go all the way." He looked around his yard and the surrounding forest. "I don't feel safe here. I'll set out some traps, so if anyone comes snooping around, we'll know. Meanwhile, let's head out to the woods and camp for the night...just as a precaution."

163

CHAPTER 38

Haruto Surrenders

Haruto strolled through the frost-covered temple garden filled with sparkling cherry trees twisted from age. The stone walls shimmered like crystalized marble, regally glistening in the morning sunlight. She wandered through the ice kingdom feeling magical, climbing a boulder to peer over the wall at the city and nuclear plant below. The meltdown seemed beyond the human capacity to fix, yet each time the Earth Sentinels had met, she forgot to ask for a healing. She wondered why.

The Voice whispered, "Haruto, learn to surrender. Your resistance is feeding the disaster, reinforcing its reality."

For the first time, Haruto passively watched the crane-supported hoses douse water over the extremely hot, melted reactors, sending plumes of steam into the air. However, it wasn't long before she felt a familiar rage rise to the surface, but instead of letting it consume her, she released her anger to the Voice, who gladly healed the darkness with light.

CHAPTER 39

Impending War

The fallen angel glanced around the group noticing the Earth Sentinels members' stress and anger. He raised his arms. Everyone became quiet, waiting for Bechard to speak. "First, let me show you the propaganda being touted over your mainstream media." He waved his hand over the crystal ball. Images appeared of reporters discussing the supernatural storms and leaders making public announcements, repeatedly stating that the Earth Sentinels were attempting to take over the world. There was no mention of the scroll with its list of demands for earth-friendly changes. The images faded away.

From the midst of the group, a shaman shouted, "You've tricked us! The world thinks we attacked without just cause!"

Bechard calmly responded, "If you see yourself as connected to the earth, then you know the world struck the first blow a long time ago." He paused, letting them think a moment before continuing, "However, I believe people will agree to our demands, once they learn about them. It's those in power who have resisted us, protecting their own selfish interests."

Haruto, still flush from her insightful conversation with the Voice, asked, "If we see ourselves as connected to the earth, doesn't this mean we are simply battling ourselves? The way the events have played out, it appears we are manifesting, empowering, the hate against us. What if we send loving thoughts to the world instead? Create a new manifestation."

The others contemplated her words. A gentle breeze brushed their faces, tempting them to alter their sails. But their anger slowly resurfaced, churning the sea, causing the fleeting thoughts of peace to sink beneath the crashing waves.

"If there was a simpler way to accomplish this, don't you think at least one of us would have thought of it by now?" Bechard smoothly answered, then addressed the crowd, "If anyone has a peaceful solution, please speak now!"

Haruto was unfazed by Bechard's patronizing words. She no longer cared if he or anyone thought she was right or wrong. She looked at Billy, smiling ever so slightly before turning her attention to the dragon tenderly resting his snout on her lap.

Billy offered his opinion, "Although our storms were not overly violent, they did create a hostile reaction, putting the tribes at risk. It's like we've opened Pandora's Box."

Bechard said, "Right now, we need to focus on protecting the tribes. We'll cease the displays of power until after this situation resolves itself."

He continued, "Now on to what we must discuss.

Governments have falsely claimed the indigenous people are trying to take over the world, but don't be discouraged. We have the power to overcome this! However, heed this warning! If your government asks you to join them in peace talks—do NOT go! They will slaughter or imprison you. The governments have vowed revenge, but do not fear, I will do everything in my power to protect you!"

Bechard looked around and said, "Could the totem animals step forward?" Animals stepped out of the crowd, birds fluttered above, retiles slithered in, and fish and marine animals swam through the air to face the fallen angel, who asked them, "Since you have the ability to act as liaisons with the earth's creatures, would you be willing to ask them to guard the tribes?" The totem animals nodded their heads. "Thank you."

Bechard spoke to the people, "Next, we need to figure a way to let the world know our true intentions. Mankind will see things very differently once they understand we want to save the planet, not control it." He turned toward Zachary. "Would you like to tell us what you've been up to?"

The young man was caught off guard. He hadn't anticipated his recent actions being called into the limelight. He slowly moved toward Bechard, studying his face, trying to determine if the fallen angel was angry with him. Zachary nervously faced the crowd, saying, "Well, I shared a copy of the scroll with a reporter, and emailed copies to different news stations. I also submitted a photo of the scroll to a blogger, but the message was intercepted by the government." He lowered his head. "Now I'm hiding out with Billy."

Bechard said, "Although I wish you had discussed it with the group first, the information is making the

167

rounds on the Internet."

To prove it, he activated the glass ball, which displayed people around the world viewing the Earth Sentinels' scroll.

Bechard smiled, proclaiming, "See! You've started something! The post has gone viral, but most people are still uninformed. Everyone! Please spread our message any way you can! Let the world know the Earth Sentinels want justice, not power!"

CHAPTER 40

The Mysterious White Ball

US Navy warships sailed out of homeports into the Atlantic and Pacific oceans, as well as ports stationed around the world, such as South Korea, the Falklands, Sierra Leone, Kenya, Guam, the UK, Diego Garcia, Guantanamo Bay, Germany, Gibraltar, Brunei, Syria and Abu Dhabi. The destroyers each towed a floating platform that held a mysterious, gigantic white ball as they cut through the waves in the seven seas. Once they reached their destinations, the warships held their positions waiting for instructions.

CHAPTER 41

Fire It Up

Aboard the USS Tomahawk, a sailor deciphered an encrypted message before handing it to the captain to read. After uttering a prayer, the leader issued the command, "Begin Operation Blackstorm."

An engineering officer pushed several buttons.

Outside the ship, the white ball on the floating platform began to glow, emitting a whirling sound.

Next, the captain relayed coordinates that the officer entered into the shipboard computer system.

The mechanism inside the gigantic white ball began shooting a high-powered microwave beam at its target—an active waterspout in a remote part of the Pacific, just big enough to overturn a fishing boat. If left alone, the waterspout would have run its course, fizzling out long before it reached shore. Instead, because of the microwave energy, its wind speed intensified.

Over the horizon, two additional white balls were activated and began firing microwave beams at the same waterspout. The trajectory pattern amplified the storm's strength, causing it to grow exponentially into a hurricane. At this point, the white balls shifted, directing the massive storm toward its intended target.

171

Chapter 42

The Biased Media

After spending a chilly night in the woods, Zachary and Billy returned to the silver bullet trailer where Billy checked the 'traps' he had set that would have been triggered if an intruder, like a government agent, had opened the front door or tossed a seat cushion.

After deeming it safe, the men sat in the warmth of the living room watching the news play non-stop clips of indigenous people angrily protesting, as well as the mishaps caused by the supernatural storms, such as the broken awnings, missing shingles on rooftops, damaged cars, and angry passengers at the airports whose flights had been delayed.

The segment switched to a reporter, who said, "Behind me is a Cherokee reservation. We can't get close enough to see if this tribe is preparing for war, but we do know that the US troops are ready to invade all nationally recognized reservations. In order to avoid military action, peace talks between the tribes' leaders and government officials must take place by noon tomorrow, otherwise the attacks are almost certain. Back to you, Steve."

The anchorman responded with the perfect amount of decorum, "Thank you. Now let's take a look at tragic events leading to what is being dubbed, 'World War III.'" Steve narrated as a video began to play, "Here you can see tribe members blocking oil company trucks trying to cross a bridge...and here's the scene after four Canadian utility workers were killed in an explosion near the Bear Claw First Nation reservation." The camera switched back to the announcer. "For those of you just joining in, we're going to replay footage of the supernatural, animal-shaped storms that struck over a hundred cities worldwide, right after these messages."

Billy clicked the remote, switching to another news program. The headline, "Domestic Terrorism, Our Biggest Threat," flashed across the screen.

An anchorwoman spoke directly into the camera, "Now let's look at the recent uprising of the tribe near the Bear Claw Lake." The scene showed the Bear Claw Tribe members refusing to leave the Canadian military base, then Chief Keme rushing toward the soldiers, but the segment cut away before the viewers could see the chief using his body as a shield to protect Cecile from the bullet that pierced his heart.

The anchorwoman said, "As you just saw, tension has been building for a while, and obviously reached a tipping point earlier. Here to discuss tribal culture is Professor Billings, who wrote the book, *The Inevitable Demise of Indigenous People.*"

The camera showed an older, white man dressed in a tweed jacket and bow tie. He smiled, acknowledging the audience.

173

The newscaster began the interview, "In your book, you mention that the only chance tribes have to survive is to integrate into society. Would you care to expand on that?"

Disgusted, Billy changed the channel. An anchorman appeared mid-sentence, "—let's hear from Amanda Morris, live on the scene in South Dakota."

Dressed in a camel-colored cashmere coat, Amanda held a microphone, bracing herself against the cold wind blowing across the open plains. "Thanks, Tom. I am standing at the battleground of Wounded Knee where the local Oglala Sioux tribe is outraged that a private investor is selling the property. The Sioux feel the land should be owned by the tribe and dispute that a private, non-native individual can sell the land where their ancestors were killed and buried. However, documents show that a Lakota couple sold the forty acres for a thousand dollars. The current owner says the tribe has threatened him, and even burned his house, museum and personal items to the ground in 1973. At the same time, Oglala Lakota militants and members of the American Indian Movement occupied the town for seventy-one days, resulting in a shootout with the FBI, and several deaths."

What the viewers didn't hear was that the land had been forcefully bought by President Woodrow Wilson in the 1930s, and redistributed as private parcels in an attempt to disrupt the tribe's collective ownership concept—with some of the land being sold to non-natives. After decades of police corruption and brutality, unfair federal policies and the 371 treaties that had been broken by the US government, the tribe fought back, resulting in an FBI intervention and shootout that left two Native

174

Americans and two federal agents dead, in addition to 12 indigenous members who were intercepted while loading supplies and never seen again.

Nearly 1,200 tribal members were arrested for this short-lived victory, which began a reign of terror on the reservation that included 61 unsolved murders, nearly 350 assaults by gunshots, stabbings, beatings, arson and cars being run off the road, as well as 562 arrests (only 15 resulted in a conviction). The "diversions" enabled the government to illegally remove rich molybdenum and uranium deposits from the nearby Gunnery Range.

But none of these events were mentioned. Instead, the camera showed the attractive reporter standing in front of a dilapidated fence decorated with weather-worn feathers and ribbons, as well as tattered t-shirts, making the burial ground seem insignificant, although it held nearly 300 Lakota men, women and children who were killed by the US Calvary, left frozen on the ground before being buried in a mass grave.

Back in the newsroom, Tom announced, "Sorry to cut away, Amanda, this just in...the US and Canada, as well as Mexico, have officially joined forces, determined to act before the tribes have a chance to use their black magic again."

Zachary and Billy looked incredulously at each other, simultaneously reiterating, "Black magic!?"

The newscaster added, "We expect more countries to participate. Stay tuned for updates and..."

What have we done? Zachary fearfully worried about the ramifications.

Disgusted, Billy was about to shut off the TV when a foghorn-like sound blared from the set and a "Hurricane

175

Warning" flashed on the screen.

The weatherman stood in front of a global map, explaining, "This is an important update. Numerous category five hurricanes are expected to make landfall within the next few days. They're predicted to hit Mexico..." A red target icon appeared on the map. "Africa, Indonesia, Australia, the Philippines and Peru." The map was covered with red targets.

The hairs on the back of Zachary's neck stood up. "Oh, my God! One's going to hit the Amazon rainforest... Conchita!" Wide-eyed and scared, he said, "We have to help her!"

CHAPTER 43

Whale Totems

Bechard, Zachary, Billy and Chief Keme were gazing into the crystal ball when Conchita arrived, stepping through an invisible doorway.

Zachary's face lit up at the sight of her.

Conchita strode toward the lanky young man.

When she reached him, he pulled her close, holding her tightly.

The men averted their gazes, giving the young lovers impromptu privacy. After what seemed a respectable amount of time, Billy coughed, trying to capture their attention. When that didn't work, he held his hands to his mouth, calling out, "Lovebirds! We're on a time crunch here!"

However, it was another voice that broke them apart. Pahtia, who had just entered the spirit realm, shouted, "CONCHITA! Get away from that boy!"

The startled young lovers stepped apart, but continued holding hands.

Pahtia stared disapprovingly at his daughter.

Billy broke the standoff by announcing, "Pahtia, there's a hurricane headed toward your jungle!"

Pahtia did not understand the importance of the statement, since the tribe had endured many such storms in his lifetime.

Bechard interjected, "It's not just a storm. It's a man-made hurricane. Come see for yourself." He waved his hand over the glass sphere, revealing the oceans obscured by swirling cloud formations. The scene magnified, dipping below the hurricane funnels, showing a Navy cruiser guarding a floating platform holding a glowing, white ball. "What you're seeing is the newest weather warfare machine developed by the US government. Creating man-made storms is inexpensive compared to other methods, and the government doesn't have to admit they attacked another country...they can simply blame it on God." He chuckled at their ingeniousness. "But this time, they plan to blame the storms on the Earth Sentinels to gain public support for the war against us."

Pahtia implored, "Why not talk to the hurricanes? Ask them to stop."

"I tried...it didn't work. Here, you try," said Bechard, motioning for the shaman to step up.

Pahtia viewed the storm inside the crystal ball, shouting, "Hello! Can you hear me!?"

The storm cried, "What's wrong with me? Help me!"

Pahtia shouted at the top of his lungs at the glass sphere, "STOP!" But the storm continued crying as if she never heard him.

Bechard explained, "The storm is overcome by the energy. After I destroy the government's machines, it should be able to hear us."

Chief Keme asked anxiously, "What about protecting the tribes from attack?"

"Of course!" Bechard responded, "We will take care of both, but first, I need to do this." He placed his hand on the glass ball. Lightning erupted, racing through the sky toward the floating platform, striking the whirling ball. Its electric fingers sizzled over the orb, but failed to penetrate the mechanism. It was as if an invisible force field protected the weapon.

Pahtia grumpily asked, "What do we do now?"

Bechard seemed perturbed until an idea popped into his head. "I know some totem spirits who might help us." He raised his arms and his blue-tipped wings expanded, making him resemble a magnificent deity. He closed his eyes, beckoning totem spirits from another realm.

A blue tint filled the air.

In the distance, whale calls echoed.

Splashing noises were heard.

Conchita's hair floated in a phantom water current while a school of fish swam in front of her. Seaweed drifted past.

Zachary tried touching a fish, but it flitted away.

A Sperm Whale spirit swam into view, followed by Humpback, Blue, Beluga and Orca spirits blowing air out their blowholes. The sound reverberated throughout the realm.

Bechard was pleased by their arrival. "Welcome! Thank you for coming. The humans have developed another method for manipulating the weather and we need your help stopping them."

The Sperm Whale was skeptical. "Why should we help?"

179

"Good question! We are trying to prevent mankind from ruining the planet. However, our power only goes so far. I tried destroying their hurricane-making machines, but the military installed a sophisticated lightning-rod system. I could overpower the machines with stronger lightning bolts, but that would electrify all the marine life within miles of the strikes."

The whales listened, contemplating whether to participate or not.

"We need to destroy the machines as soon as possible!" Bechard declared. "Will you help us?"

CHAPTER 44

The World's Response

The US president walked down a red-carpeted hallway, stopping at a podium with the official seal of the United States affixed to the front. He spoke into the camera, "Good afternoon, fellow Americans. For the past month, the world has been experiencing supernatural storms, but these events were minor compared to the devastation about to unfold. Level five hurricanes currently headed toward Peru, Mexico, Africa, Indonesia, Australia and the Philippines are about to cause unimaginable property damage and loss of life. It goes without saying, these countries have our heartfelt prayers and support.

"Our intelligence agencies and allies have confirmed that these storms were created by the geo-terrorists known as the Earth Sentinels, a group of indigenous people from around the world. This unfortunately includes our own North American tribes.

"In a humanitarian effort, we offered the US tribes an opportunity to relocate into monitored communities... an offer they steadfastly rejected. And while this country has supported their freedoms in the past, the indigenous tribes have resisted assimilating into our society. The Earth Sentinels' attacks have left us no choice but to take forceful action against them. May God have mercy on their souls."

In the Congo, the prime minister fumed over the betrayal by his trusted advisor, confident that the shaman knew in advance about the hurricane headed his way. Now the people were rallying against him, thinking he was cursed. *I need to demonstrate that I have control over this situation,* the prime minister thought, pondering a solution. He yelled for his butler, who quickly responded, stopping obediently at the dining room entrance, waiting for his instructions. "Tell Manyara to come here."

132

A few minutes later, the out-of-breath driver appeared holding his cap between his hands. "Sir, you asked for me?"

"You drove a man, a shaman, home last month. Remember?"

"Yes, well...actually, I didn't drive him home. After a few miles, he got out. Said he wanted to walk the rest of—"

The prime minster screamed, "I asked you to do one thing! One thing!"

The driver lowered his head. "I couldn't force him to—"

"Get out!" the prime minister commanded, watching the driver scurry down the hall before making a phone call to his deputy minister. "Lionel? I need you to get me a dozen prisoners who were sentenced for witchcraft." He paused to listen. "Because we're going to make examples out of them."

In Russia, the president glared over the city, trying to figure out how to round up the shamans responsible for the current predicament. During the 1920s, Russians went on a bloody rampage killing all known shamans. In the early 1980s, the government officially announced there were no more shamans alive in its country.

Do I admit there are shamans? Or do I blame the storms on shamans from other countries that foolishly let them live? The president contemplated his choices, finally deciding, *Let the other countries do the dirty work. What few shamans we have left couldn't possibly have created these disasters.*

Japan had a very different response than most of the world. With its history of integrating shamans into the ruling class and preoccupation with the Fukushima nuclear meltdown, the government didn't plan an attack on the Miko and Geki. However, they did see an opportunity to blame them for the nuclear disaster. A public mandate was issued, demanding that the female and male shamans turn themselves in to the authorities.

Haruto and the other women living at the temple were not fools. Instead, they quickly transformed the temple into a yoga and meditation studio, hanging a new sign and placing ads in the local paper. Oddly enough, business picked up.

Chapter 45

Inside the Rez

The community center was packed to the brim with mournful tribe members. Cecile stood at the front and said with a heavy heart, "It's time to begin. Tom, would you please lead us in prayer?"

Accepting the invitation, he bowed his head, uttering the words, "*Nohtawinan Kisemanito.* Keep us this day. We need your guidance during this difficult time. We face death at the hands of a cruel government. We do not expect to win this fight, but we do expect to die with honor. We ask that you embrace our women and children, and welcome our fallen warriors. *Kita-tamihinan.*"

After a moment of silence, Cecile began the meeting, "First on the agenda, our children's safety. Do we accept the government's offer to send them to detention camps or keep them with us, facing possible death? If sent away, will the government treat them harshly? When they are grown, where will they live? Work? There's nowhere to go, the world hates us."

The silence was deafening as the severity of the situation

set in. Some remembered their childhoods when they were forced into the residential school system that forbade the practice of their native customs and taught them the ways of the white man. With a Bible in one hand and a stick in the other, the teachers beat and abused them. Over a third of the children died during their "education". Most were buried in the cemeteries located on school property. Those who weren't subjected to the school system heard the horror stories from their parents and grandparents.

Tom asked, "Should we send our children into the hands of a corrupt government? With the adults all gone, who will be there for the little ones? If they make it out alive. Who will explain to them it wasn't their fault? Who will explain that no one really understands the ways of the white man, not even the white man?"

A mother shouted, "If the truth comes out, our children will have a place in the world!"

185

A skeptical old man shook his head, disagreeing, "We've experienced centuries of genocide, and the truth still remains hidden."

Grandma Hausis suggested, "What if we don't run or fight, but sit peacefully with our children? The soldiers would have to look us in the eyes to shoot us!"

"Noooo! I want my babies to live!" a mother cried. The woman next to her comforted her.

Tears ran down many stoic faces.

A teenage girl burst through the double doors at the back of the meeting room, her form silhouetted by rays of sun streaming through the doorway.

Everyone turned around.

She shouted, "Come quick!" motioning with her arm.

The tribe members rushed out the doors expecting

the worse, but instead, the tribe stood in wonder at the sight before them.

Filtering out of the forest, hundreds of wild animals were promenading through the village. At the forefront of the patchwork group were fierce grizzlies and black bears, snorting and grunting, causing the children to cling to their parents, partly out of fear, but mostly in awe as they watched the magnificent beasts lumber in unison. Stepping behind them were herds of deer and elk. Next came gray lynx with tufted ears and bobbed tails, padding alongside silver wolves and golden cougars. The ground shuddered as the bison's hooves hit the dirt, churning up dust. Behind the great beasts were red foxes marching with beavers, followed by moose taking long strides. At the end of the line, masked wolverines scampered beside coyotes while majestic bald eagles and hawks soared overhead.

When the creatures reached the edge of the houses, they split into two groups, filing left and right around the perimeters of the village, ready to protect the tribe against the encroaching Canadian Army.

Tom turned to Cecile and said, "Well, this puts a new spin on things! I'm going to make a phone call. It's time the world knew the truth!"

CHAPTER 46

Reconnaissance Missions

While the Canadian armed forces ramped up for battle, an Air Force pilot flew at low altitude over the Bear Claw First Nation territory conducting reconnaissance. The pilot was stunned to see predators and prey aligned together, creating a barrier around the tribe's territory. He circled twice before he radioed in, "We got a situation. It appears there are wild animals protecting the Bear Claw Tribe. Anyone else seeing this?"

Flying over the Huron territory, a pilot answered in a voice riddled with static, "For sure! Same here. Bears, moose, wolves. Man, those will make great trophies!"

The pilots spun their jets around, heading back to the base.

A Peruvian military helicopter flew over the Amazon jungle searching for indigenous villages, but the dense forest canopy hid all signs of life.

The pilot spoke into his helmet's microphone, "What do you think the chances are of spotting one tribe, much less all of them?"

The co-pilot responded, "Don't know why we're bothering. The hurricane will wipe 'em out. We should just let nature take its course."

"Doesn't it seem strange that the tribes would create storms against themselves?" the pilot asked, surveying the landscape.

The co-pilot shrugged his shoulders, then resumed studying the rainforest below.

CHAPTER 47

The Mess Hall

Three US Navy sailors were watching television in the ship's mess hall when a weather warning interrupted their program. A meteorologist showed the latest radar maps of the Category 5 hurricanes raging around the globe.

One of the sailors exclaimed, "Wow! Those storms are fucking huge! Those natives give me the heebie-jeebies."

"Did you hear about Lieutenant Martinez and Private Locklear being locked in the brig?" the second sailor asked. "Both said they wouldn't fight their own people."

"That's the problem with these minorities—they need to learn how to be Americans first."

The third sailor piped in, "Man, they were here first!"

"Yeah, a thousand years ago! Say, did you check out that white ball next to our ship?"

The other men nodded their heads.

"What do you think it is?"

"I have no idea, and frankly, I don't want to know. The Navy don't pay me to think."

"Ding, ding, ding! We have a winner!"

"Funny, asshole."

The first sailor yelled, "Shut up! I can't hear the TV!"

CREAK!

"What the hell was that!?" exclaimed the first sailor.

A moan echoed from the bowels of the ship, sending vibrations throughout the vessel, which lurched.

The sailors grabbed their drinks before they spilled, assuming the ship would return to its upright position, however, it continued tipping. They fell out of the chairs that were bolted to the floor, hitting the wall with a bang.

"Get above! We're sinking!" the second sailor yelled, holding his ribs.

Underneath the warship, whales pushed the keel of the boat sideways and upward. The ship's metal structure groaned as the whales used their massive strength to build momentum, swinging the ship's bottom to the surface, tilting the destroyer on its side.

The whales surfaced for air, their soulful eyes peering at the shipwreck and the radiant white ball floating nearby, then they swam away.

With half of the cruiser's deck submerged in the ocean, the interior rapidly took on water. The sailors in the mess hall desperately tried to reach the narrow staircase. The first sailor grabbed the railing, but it was too late.

A wave swelled at the top of the staircase, rushing down, plunging him backwards.

The salt water quickly filled the room, creating a strong undertow that pulled the men under, banging them against the walls, floor and fixed furnishings until they drowned.

Their lifeless bodies flowed with the current into the next compartment.

Sailors who had been working on the deck were flung into the sea where they now fought against the waves, swimming toward the rubber rafts that had automatically dispatched when the equilibrium of the ship shifted.

The survivors climbed into the lifeboats, watching the war cruiser sink below the surface, heading toward the bottom of the sea with the remaining crew trapped inside the hull of the gray tomb.

The cable attached to the floating platform became taut, dragging the mysterious ball across the water. When it reached the spot where the ship went under, the platform tipped on its side, just long enough to shoot a misdirected microwave beam across the rubber rafts, burning the casing and killing some of the sailors, then it disappeared beneath the waves, heading toward the sea floor, its metal structure groaning as the oceanic pressure increased. The cable to the white ball snapped. The light flickered off and the whirling mechanism finally stopped.

191

Meanwhile, the burnt lifeboats, which had been turned into remnants of useless rubber sheets, churned in the waves.

Charred, dead bodies floated on the surface beside the still-living sailors, who desperately treaded water.

It didn't take long for the sharks to appear.

Chapter 48

Talking with Hurricanes

With the white balls eliminated, the shamans were able to communicate with the man-made hurricanes. Over the course of several days, the shamans persuaded the storms to deescalate into gentler tropical storms or head out to sea where they dissipated, saving millions of lives and preventing needless pain and suffering.

CHAPTER 49

Interviewing Tom

"Hello, Channel Five News. How may I direct your call?"

"I'd like to speak to a reporter," Tom said.

"One moment, please."

A prerecorded infomercial played while he waited. "For the latest in news, weather and sports, tune into Channel Five News, always the latest, always what's important to—"

"Hello, this is Bill, can I help you?"

"This is Tom Running Deer, I'm a councilman in the Bear Claw Tribe—"

"Yes! We're reporting live near your reservation!"

"I know—anyway, before the army invades, I need to get our message out. I just sent you an email. It contains a photo of the Earth Sentinels' scroll. Take a look. If a reporter can get here in the next five minutes, we *might* have time to talk. I'll be waiting." He hung up.

Bill immediately called their onsite reporter, Lisa Bantoné, whose crew was parked on a bluff overlooking the tribe's village.

Lisa answered her cell phone, "Hello?" She listened and a smile spread across her face. She blurted, "Will do!" then shouted, "Let's go, boys!"

The news van sped down the dirt road, slowing as it neared the entrance guarded by wild animals. As promised, Tom was waiting, but because he stood between a grizzly bear and bison, nobody wanted to get out of the vehicle. The satellite antenna on the roof extended.

Lisa refused to let this opportunity slip by her. She rolled down the window, waving Tom over.

Tom walked up to the van.

"Hi! I'm Lisa Bantoné. Since we're short on time, let's get to it. For the record, would you mind introducing yourself?" She held her microphone out the window. The cameraman crouched next to Lisa's seat, focusing on Tom.

"I'm Tom Running Deer, a councilman in the Bear Claw First Nation Tribe. I want the world to know the truth before it's too late. While I can't speak for all the tribes, mine is proud to be a part of the Earth Sentinels. Our mission was, and still is, to stop people from destroying Mother Earth.

"The Earth Sentinels did create the lightning storms, but those were to get attention for our cause, not hurt anyone. However...we're not responsible for the hurricanes." He shouted, "I repeat, we are NOT responsible for the hurricanes!" Tom calmed down, continuing, "Anyway, to better understand our mission, go online and search for the Earth Sentinels' scroll. You'll see that our demands were not for power, and that we didn't mean to threaten your lives. We just wanted people to use earth-friendly methods, making the world a better place for *all* of us."

A military plane buzzed overhead, drowning out Tom's voice as it took a wide swoop around the village.

Army tanks and vehicles appeared on the horizon.

Without saying another word, Tom walked back toward his people—to the men, women and children who sat in a circle with their backs to the world, guarded by wild animals.

CHAPTER 50

Chief Red Sun Speaks

Zachary's parents sat in the living room anxiously watching the news coverage of the war against the Earth Sentinels.

An anchorman announced, "We're on the phone with Chief Red Sun from the Navajo Nation in Arizona. I believe you have something to say...please, go ahead."

The gruff voice of an old man was heard, "The Navajo are a gentle people who have been oppressed since the white man first came to this land, centuries ago. Despite this, our young men fought during World War II, used our sacred language to relay tactical information, keeping it secret from this country's enemies, and they fought in many wars since. Still, you continue to hunt us."

"Sir, um, I mean Chief Red Sun, didn't the Earth Sentinels attack the world first?"

"You narrowly define attack. To our people, every time a forest is cut down, it is an attack against us. Every time toxic chemicals are dumped in a river, it is an attack against us. We see ourselves as part of the earth. When she is attacked, we are attacked. However, we are not Earth Sentinels."

"So you're saying that you don't support the Earth Sentinels?" the reporter asked.

"We support their goals."

"Have you seen the infamous scroll making its rounds on the Internet?" the reporter inquired. A photo of the scroll appeared on the screen.

Yelling was heard off screen.

The line went dead.

"Hello? Hello?" the reporter asked. "I guess we lost our connection. Next, we'll hear from Chief Toméz."

Marilyn laid her head on her husband's chest and cried, afraid for her son.

Larry gently stroked her hair. "I can't say he'll be fine, but I know I've never been prouder of him than I am right now."

CHAPTER 51

The War Begins

Military helicopters flew toward the Bear Claw tribal territory, descending from the sky like a swarm of locusts ready to consume its human harvest. The gunners crouched near the open doors while the pilots kept their eyes on the approaching reservation, not knowing that above them black clouds were gathering, spinning faster and faster, evolving into tornadoes. The dark funnels gained speed and began chasing the helicopters.

A gunman shouted at the pilot, "Sir! Twisters at 12 o'clock!"

The pilot leaned closer to the windshield, peering at the sky above. He swore under his breath, then thrust the joystick downward, trying to outmaneuver the fast-approaching funnel clouds, but it was too late. One of the tornadoes tugged the helicopter backwards, causing it to wobble, spinning out of control. The gunners tried to hold on, but they lost their grips and tumbled out. The rotary blades sliced the men faster than a sushi chef.

The swarm of tornadoes enveloped the remaining

helicopters, crumpling their rotary wings and tail sections like paper airplanes. Then without warning, the twisters dissipated, letting the damaged machines free fall from the sky, crashing to the ground. Fireballs burst over the landscape.

A military convoy of M35 covered trucks, armored vehicles and tanks, as well as buses meant for transporting the children and prisoners of war, approached the tribe's village, but came to a stop as a blizzard blew in, swirling around them, intensifying until all visibility was lost. The soldiers were trapped inside the vehicles, left to wait out the storm.

On the opposite side of the Bear Claw territory, a Special Forces sniper team was sneaking up on the tribe, stealthily scouting for an advantageous location, unaware of the isolated blizzard on the other side of the forest. The men found a hill overlooking the houses, then hunkered down next to the trees, taking their positions.

199

One of the men slapped the back of his neck, examining his hand. "Funny, there's still mosquitoes this time of the year, eh?"

"Yah, maybe they migrated from that balmy state of Montana." The soldier chuckled.

"Damnit, again!"

Another man smacked his own forehead. "Wow! Testy little suckers, aren't they, eh?"

"Shit, they're everywhere!"

The men swatted their arms, feverishly batting at the swarm of mosquitoes buzzing around them. The blood-thirsty insects bit the men's faces, eyes, nostrils, ears and eyelids, as well as through their uniforms.

The soldiers fled, leaving their equipment behind.

They were out of breath by the time they stopped in the woods, glancing around to see if they had outrun the aggressive insects.

One of the men huffed, "This place is cursed," spitting bugs out of his mouth.

Welts formed on their faces.

A twig snapped. The men reached for the guns they no longer held. Fear slipped over them. Dozens of glowing eyes stared at them from the shadows. Bears and wolves stepped out from the trees, methodically moving toward the men who turned to run, only to discover that lynx and cougars stood in their way.

The Bear Claw tribe was sitting around the bonfire when they heard screams echoing from the forest.

In Arizona, a Navajo tribe stoically waited for the US forces to arrive. Their reservation was located in a desert dotted with succulent plants and cacti. In the distance stood picturesque sandstone rocks overlooking canyons, which had been gently carved over countless millenniums. The tribe members sat together in the shade under the Pueblo-styled pavilion communing with the Great Spirit.

In the midst of the desert's heat, an army convoy drove down a desolate highway, stopping outside the reservation. The armored trucks and tanks idled their engines while the squad leaders sat in a Humvee studying the wild animals.

"That is the strangest thing I've ever seen," said the second-in-command.

"Stranger than animal-shaped storms!? Come on, let's round 'em up before it gets any weirder," instructed the platoon leader who rolled down his window, shouting through a megaphone, "This is your last chance to surrender your children! They won't be harmed! Send out your children!"

While they waited for a response, fire ants emerged out of the ground. Undetected, the insects scurried over the vehicles, moving through the cracks in the metal doors, sneaking inside. The ants moved swiftly toward the soldiers, dashing across the floor and over the seats. The vicious insects crept under the soldiers' uniforms, covering their bodies, but they did not bite immediately. The ants waited for the telepathic command, then simultaneously clamped down on men's skin, injecting them with venom. The pain was excruciating. The soldiers screamed, batting their bodies trying to kill the ants, but more poured in, crawling inside the men's ears, nostrils and mouths, and stinging their genitals. The men scrambled out of the vehicles, attempting to escape, but, to their horror, found themselves swarmed by killer bees and meat-eating yellow jackets.

Hundreds of attacks occurred around the world. Some of the tribes fought back while others sat peacefully. Regardless of their responses, wild creatures and supernatural weather phenomena protected each tribe.

201

CHAPTER 52

Double-Edged Sword

A very unhappy US president confronted his generals. "Well, gentlemen, someone want to explain why we're failing so miserably in a war against people with little more than shotguns and Molotov cocktails?"

A commanding general spoke first, "That's not quite true, sir. They also have wild animals and supernatural powers protecting them. Our weapons and manpower are no match for them."

"How about a different approach?"

"Such as?"

"You know..."

"You mean chemical warfare?"

"No! That's too obvious! I'm talking about good old-fashioned germs. There must be something in our vaults. Spanish flu...yellow fever?"

"That's dangerous stuff and could easily spread to the public!"

"Not if we keep 'em rounded up."

Another general said, "If the media or United Nations

find out, they'll crucify us! Look, we have a stalemate in this war. No forces anywhere have been able to infiltrate a single tribe—"

"Here's an idea," Bechard interrupted.

The men gasped, spooked by the sudden appearance of the fallen angel lounging on the couch with his arm propped over the back and his blue-tipped wings pressed against the cushions. His blue robe was elegantly draped over his crossed legs.

Bechard coldly smiled. "Why don't you retreat? You're not going to win." His piercing aquamarine eyes struck terror in each man's heart. "I'm tired of this game. Would you like to die from yellow fever? Or perhaps your wives and children? It could be arranged." He heard the men's hearts pounding and knew their throats were tight from fear. "Just as I thought. Not so fun when the gun is aimed at you, is it?

"You have until tomorrow at noon to announce that the Earth Sentinels pose no threat to the world. And afterward, no harassing our members, no agents sitting outside their doors, no blacklists, and, most of all, no assassinations. Is that clear?"

The president and his men nodded.

"I'll let you decide whether to mention our list of demands in your speech tomorrow. But I warn you...public awareness is growing, and if change doesn't happen soon, we'll resume our mission. One more thing, pull back those troops immediately or the Earth Sentinels will create displays of power that make the previous ones look like child's play."

The fallen angel got up. "Well...got to go, so much to do and so little time." Then he disappeared before their eyes.

203

CHAPTER 53

The Retreat

After the blizzard ceased, the Bear Claw Tribe members watched the armored vehicles maneuver over the snow-covered terrain, disappearing into the horizon. With the threat gone, the wild animals ambled away, fading into the forest.

A wave of relief and gratitude spread over the people. Cecile prayed out loud, "Thank you, Great Spirit! We are thankful to spend another day in each other's company. Forgive us for our attacks. Forgive us for trying to change the world. We can do nothing more than change ourselves."

Tom lit a sage bundle, then motioned for the people to come forward one by one. They each took turns standing in front of him, letting the smoke rise over their bodies, taking their negative energy to the heavens for purification.

CHAPTER 54

Declaration of Peace

The lawmakers applauded as the President of the United States stepped up to the podium, ready to address the nation. Behind him were the party leaders showing their support. The president cleared his throat, reading from the teleprompter, "I'm happy to announce that we have reached a ceasefire agreement with the Earth Sentinels. All the US military troops stationed near the Native American reservations have returned to their bases. This peaceful resolution was made possible through the heroic efforts of our top advisors speaking directly with the Earth Sentinels' leader."

The politicians clapped.

"During the negotiations, it became clear that their mission was to save the planet from imminent destruction caused by the world's misuse of its natural resources, plants and animals.

"Although we don't condone the Earth Sentinels' actions, there is a need for change. Fossil fuels won't last forever, and innovations in alternative fuel sources are crucial to maintaining our way of life, solving our fuel shortages and creating jobs we can be proud of. And one day, when renewable fuels are commonplace, their costs will decrease, meaning all Americans will have more money in their pockets!"

Everyone applauded. A few members from the president's party cheered.

"So, we're going to put aside our differences and continue meeting with the Native American tribes to rebuild our relationship. I urge you to do the same. Let's not hold grudges. That will only keep us stuck in the past...and this country is ready to move forward!"

The politicians politely clapped.

"I realize change is never easy! It will take an effort by every American, as well as lawmakers working together across party lines to build our country's future!"

The congressional men and women applauded, giving the appearance of a unified front.

The president smiled, nodding his head appreciatively. "I truly believe this recent confrontation has helped all of us to become more aware of the urgent need to find better ways to heat our homes, fuel our cars, grow our food and humanely raise animals. These changes will make the world a better place for all of us, for generations to come. God bless you and your family."

He received a standing ovation.

The Prime Minister of the Democratic Republic of the Congo gave his speech from an undisclosed location for his own safety, because the people thought he was cursed by black magic. The recent public hanging of 12 witches did little to improve his approval ratings. Yet, he knew that meeting the Earth Sentinels' list of demands was necessary, because if the group created any more supernatural weather phenomena, his people would most likely hang him in the public square.

Damn that traitor shaman! he seethed.

Canada's prime minister was infuriated, casting blame for the whole Earth Sentinels disaster onto America who, in his mind, had accelerated the events into a war. Now he had to explain the disastrous attacks to the House of Commons and Senate in a discovery session later in the day. Meanwhile, thousands of angry demonstrators were protesting in front of the Centre Block building. It was not going to be a good day.

Chapter 55

The Homecoming

Marilyn was making dinner in the kitchen. The dogs rested under the table, keeping a keen eye out for falling scraps. The back door creaked as someone opened it, causing the dogs to spring to life, barking wildly.

Zachary stepped inside, grinning from ear to ear at the sight of his mother.

She set down her paring knife, rushing to greet him, nearly tripping over one of the dogs. She cried tears of joy as she hugged her son, kissing his forehead, then hugging him again tightly. "It's so good to see you! I'm so glad you're all right! I've got to let your father know! He's been so worried about you."

"Let me," he requested.

She stepped back, taking a good look at him. "I guess I'll let you go." She laughed giddily. "He's in the barn."

Zachary stepped outside, walking across the backyard with the dogs romping around him. The family cow mooed, ambling closer to the fence, hoping for a treat or head scratch.

The barn door was open. Inside, his father was cleaning

a stall. The dogs ran in, nipping at each other playfully.

Larry looked over to see what was going on. He saw his son. "Zach!" He dropped the shovel and rushed toward him. They held each other for a moment. "I'm so glad you're okay! You're okay, right?"

Zachary nodded.

"Wonderful! You have to tell me all about it!" Larry kept his arm around him as they ambled toward the house.

During dinner, Zachary began telling his parents the story of the Earth Sentinels. It was nearly midnight before he broke the news, "Mom...Dad...I know this is unorthodox, but I'd like to use my college funds to travel."

His parents sat shocked, not sure what to say.

Larry gained his composure, cleared his throat, then asked, "Where to?"

Chapter 56

The Grocery Store

With her hands tucked in her coat pockets, Cecile trudged through the slush to stand on Tom's makeshift porch. She knocked on his door that badly needed a new coat of paint.

After a moment, Tom opened the door, surprised to see her. "Hey! What's up?" he asked, noticing that she was driving the community van.

She sheepishly answered with a question, "Wanna go get groceries with me?"

He scoffed. "Strange first date."

"It's not a date!"

"Um, hmm."

Exasperated, Cecile explained, "Neechie, this is the first time since the attacks, and I don't know…"

Tom understood her fear. "Sure. Let me grab my coat."

Cecile and Tom drove out of the village, heading down the isolated dirt road, passing farm fields nipped by frost, lined with barren trees asleep until spring, blanketed by an overcast sky.

When they reached the next field, she became solemn. Several oil rigs were pumping and a new one was under construction. She felt her anger rise to the surface, but instead of letting it consume her, she offered it to the Great Spirit, silently praying, *Please take this unloving thought from me...I don't want it anymore.*

Ahead, protestors obstructed the road. Police cars were stationed nearby. Cecile slowed down, examining the men and women holding signs with the words, "Falicon Frack Off!" "Keep It in the Ground," and "We Support the Earth Sentinels!" The last sign surprised her.

When the protestors saw the indigenous man and woman inside the vehicle, they stepped out of the way, allowing them to pass. Cecile inched forward, past the police officers, past the demonstrators who shouted, "Earth Sentinels! Earth Sentinels! Earth Sentinels!" She and Tom nodded their heads in solidarity.

Picking up speed, Cecile said, "I don't want to fight anymore," glancing at the people in her rearview mirror.

Tom reached over, holding her hand. "There's a time for war, a time for peace...and a time for love." Out of the corner of her eye, Cecile saw him slyly grin and wiggle his eyebrows. She hit the gas, suddenly in a hurry. There were groceries to buy, bread to fry and love to be made!

211

CHAPTER 57

India

At a makeshift airport in the heart of India's Cotton Belt, Zachary stepped off a prop plane. The heat and smell were overpowering. His exhausted father and mother trailed behind him.

Marilyn haggardly suggested, "Let's get a taxi and go to the hotel. I need to lie down," mopping the sweat from her forehead with a napkin.

They entered a small, unairconditioned building painted bright yellow that served as the terminal. A friendly porter wearing a formal, long sherwani greeted them.

He clasped his hands and bowed his head slightly, saying, "Good day, sirs and lady. I will gladly find you a taxi, okay?"

Larry and Marilyn nodded.

The porter walked out the entranceway to the street. He whistled. Seconds later, a glorified golf cart swung to the curb. The porter motioned that this was their ride, hurrying back to grab their luggage.

Marilyn glanced at the taxi before whispering to Larry, "I don't think we're going to fit in that."

Zachary and his parents waited in the shade while the driver and porter feverishly secured the luggage, tying some of the bags to the back, piling the rest on the roof. The driver tightened the strap and the porter waved them over. Marilyn slid into the backseat, causing the luggage on top to sway dangerously. Larry gingerly got in, sitting beside his wife. Zachary took the seat next to the driver.

The taxi weaved through the busy streets where the open-air vendors called out their wares. Dogs and children roamed freely. The hodgepodge storefronts were built in a wide array of sizes, painted multiple colors with banners and signs hanging to and fro.

The driver introduced himself, "I am Harsha. I take you to hotel not far from here."

213

Zachary saw a woman cooking beside the street and peddlers pushing carts. A small boy in dirty clothes ran alongside the taxi begging for change, but before Zachary could pull out his wallet, the boy was left behind with his palm still extended. Zachary asked the driver to stop.

The driver shook his head. "We not stop. They will take your things. We must keep going."

When they arrived at the hotel, the family got out of the taxi, entering the compact lobby. Every inch of the walls was covered with ornate, painted motifs and framed pictures. A tarnished brass-and-crystal chandelier hung in the high-arched ceiling over the well-worn Queen Anne furniture.

The proprietor greeted them at the counter, "Welcome to our humble abode!" He paused, noticing that Marilyn was sweating profusely. "Madam, please sit down. We will bring water to you, okay?" He clapped, shouting at the houseboy who was heading outside to retrieve the luggage, "Quick! Bring her bottled water!"

The houseboy spun around, leaving the taxi driver to manage on his own.

After the luggage was placed on the rolling cart, the proprietor escorted them to their rooms. He paraded them along a balcony overlooking the courtyard, which featured a fish pond surrounded by lounge chairs and urns overflowing with ferns. The stucco walls facing the courtyard were painted with fresco botanical decorations. The Thompson family had stumbled upon an oasis in the middle of the city.

214

The next morning, Zachary and his parents rode in a rickshaw. The driver slowly pedaled down the street filled with beggars—mothers with children, children without mothers, the disabled, the blind and the old. Some lay on the ground too weak to sit.

"Are you sure you'll recognize them?" Marilyn asked, overwhelmed by the misery.

"Yes," said Zachary, searching for Mahakanta Suresh's family. A group of boys ran up to the rickshaw. This time Zachary was prepared, dropping money into their outstretched hands.

The driver slowed at an intersection. On the corner was a temple decorated with stonework painted yellow ocher and orange. A mother and her two daughters and son sat under a papaya tree eating its fruit. They were thin, dirty and shabbily dressed.

"Over there!" Zachary yelled, pointing to the spot.

The driver pulled to the curb.

Zachary got out.

The mother and children stared at the Westerner.

It suddenly dawned on Zachary that explaining his presence might not be as easy as he had imagined.

The young girls rushed over to him, begging, "Please! Please!"

He gave them money, moving toward the mother. "Are you the wife of Mahakanta Suresh?"

She did not speak English, but she did recognize her husband's name.

Her son spoke on her behalf, "He is my father."

"Your father sent me to help you."

"My father is dead."

"I know. I'm sorry. Have you heard of the Earth Sentinels?"

"The storm creators?"

"Yes, exactly. I am part of the Earth Sentinels and so is your father. He and the other farmers who committed... um...died...have joined us."

The boy's throat tightened as he tried not to cry.

"Please tell your mother that your father asked me to buy back your farm...for you, for your family."

Overcome with emotion, the boy put his hand to his mouth. He relayed the information to his mother. She listened attentively. Tears welled up in her eyes. Speaking in Hindi, she discussed the unexpected turn of events with her son. The boy shrugged his shoulders. The mother studied Zachary, glancing at his parents sitting in the rickshaw, then instructed her son to ask a question.

"How do we know you are friends with the spirit of my father?"

215

"He told me there is a silver bell hidden in the dirt floor under the window. He buried it as a child, thinking it would bring luck. But does it matter? I'm offering your life back. Take it!"

The boy discussed the news with his mother. She nodded. He relayed her decision, "We will take it."

CHAPTER 58

Mahakanta's Farm

Eight people, including the driver, were packed inside a mid-size taxi speeding toward Mahakanta's farm. Farmers in the fields watched the yellow car drive by, leaving a trail of dust. When they reached the farm, the driver parked in the shade of an old banyan tree. Everyone got out, stretching their legs. The girls ran around the house playing. A neighbor woman came over to greet Mahakanta's wife, who cried with happiness at seeing a familiar face.

With Zachary beside him, Mahakanta's son walked into the empty house. The teary-eyed boy proceeded to the window where a ray of sunshine marked the spot. He hunkered down, digging in the soil with his bare hands. Faster and faster he dug, suddenly stopping. Gently probing with his fingers, he pulled out a rusty tin. Holding his breath, he opened the lid, peering inside. A tarnished silver bell was inside. He stared in amazement at the symbol of his father's past hope. Tears ran down his cheeks as he held it close to his heart.

Zachary left the house to give the boy privacy. When he stepped outside, Marilyn, Larry and Mahakanta's wife stared at him, anxiously waiting for him to indicate whether the bell had been found or not. He nodded.

The wife raised her arms, shouting at the sky in her native tongue, "Thank you, Mahakanta!"

The moneylenders came the next day, meeting with Zachary's parents to settle the debt for $825 in US dollars —a paltry sum by American standards. In addition, the Thompsons gave Mahakanta's family money to buy traditional seeds, a pair of oxen, a cart, and still have enough left over for a tough season. It was agreed that they would never use the "magic seeds" again.

CHAPTER 59

Japan

Smoking a long-stemmed pipe, Haruto gazed out the window. Her thoughts were interrupted when a young woman informed her that the next client had arrived. Haruto nodded, walking over to a table set against the back wall. There, she emptied the tobacco from her pipe into a brass urn, closing the lid to seal in the smoke.

A man strolled through the door, standing boldly in the middle of the room. "Nice place you got here, Haruto."

Recognizing the voice, she spun around. Overcome with emotion, she rushed toward Billy and he moved toward her. They came together, embracing. Billy stepped back and peered into her eyes. "You're even more beautiful in person."

"How did you find me?" asked Haruto in stilted English, astounded by his presence.

He took out his wallet, pulling out a piece of torn newspaper. Printed on it was an advertisement featuring the grand opening of the yoga and meditation center, complete with photos of the Mikos. "Very twenty-first century!" he commented, "And nice photo! I see some of the women offer massages. I might get one of those!"

Haruto smacked him on the arm. "I will be the only one giving you massage!" she insisted, then blushed, realizing the implication of her words.

Without saying a word, Billy went to the door and locked it. With a devilish gleam in his eyes, he returned to her, sweeping her into his arms, kissing her passionately.

Outside the temple, the birds sang, ignoring the devastated nuclear plant billowing steam in the distance.

CHAPTER 60

Searching for Conchita

In the farmhouse kitchen, Zachary sat at the table with his parents explaining his newest plan.

Larry reiterated, "Let me see if I've got this right. After you turn eighteen, you want to go to Peru and wander through a rainforest filled with hostile tribes that have never seen a white man to search for Conchita. By yourself!"

"Yes! She'll have her father spread the word among the tribes to keep an eye out for a light-skinned young man...asking them not to hurt me."

"Son, I'm beginning to think you have a death wish."

"I like to think of it as not being afraid to live!"

Thirty-nine days later, a toucan warily studied Zachary and his two hired guides traveling through the rainforest. The guides were a last-minute addition, which so far had proven to be a good decision. The men were familiar with the forest, provided protection, and spoke both English and the native tongue. Zachary carried a backpack stuffed with life-saving gadgets, as well as a mini popup tent that the guides found humorous.

It had been three days since they first set out into the jungle, and although the heat and humidity were oppressive, they were fortunate it was the dry season, because that meant there were fewer mosquitoes and the trails were more accessible.

A monkey hooted. Leaves rustled. The guides warily scanned their surroundings.

Through the forest, a shout echoed, "Zach...car...ree!" Conchita stepped out of the shadows with a baby monkey perched on her shoulder. Next to her was Pahtia and three tribesmen with painted faces holding spears.

Zachary's heart skipped a beat, overwhelmed with excitement and relief at finding Conchita, but fearful of the men staring menacingly at him.

Thump. Something hit Zachary on the head. A piece of fruit bounced on the ground. Rubbing his head, he peered into the trees searching for the culprit.

A Capuchin monkey with a scar across his face sat on a branch hooting and pointing.

Conchita and the men laughed at the primate's mischievous spirit.

Zachary ignored the hostile fruit tosser and set down his backpack. Gathering his courage, he walked past the men to approach Conchita. The baby monkey jumped to Pahtia's shoulder as Zachary leaned in to kiss Conchita on the cheek, wrapping his arms around her, silently thanking the universe for manifesting his greatest desire.

Pahtia shouted a command. Startled, Zachary let go of Conchita. Pahtia repeated the command, but Zachary couldn't understand him. Without the benefit of the spirit realm, they weren't able to communicate.

One of the guides translated Pahtia's words, "He said, 'You get married today or go away.'"

Zachary glanced at Conchita, who smiled shyly, then he looked back at the trail. Thoughts of never seeing his parents again or enjoying modern conveniences ran through his mind. *Phones, refrigerators, video games, cars.* But the jungle's lush foliage, exotic birds and monkeys beckoned him—although the fruit tosser was a dubious character. At that moment, Zachary knew he would never be happy sitting in a college classroom or working in a cubicle. He turned his head toward Conchita and smiled. To demonstrate his acceptance of the "proposal", he kissed Conchita on the lips.

The men cheered! There would be a celebration tonight!

The two guides bid him farewell.

"Wait!" Zachary rummaged through his backpack, pulling out an envelope and a sheet of paper. He took a minute to jot down a message, then sealed it in an envelope, handing it to one of the guides along with some money, asking him to mail it when he returned to town.

The guide nodded his head.

Zachary watched the guides disappear into the jungle, heading back to the outside world. For a brief second, he was tempted to follow them, but when he turned around, admiring his beautiful bride-to-be, the urge passed. He clasped her hand, ready to begin a new life in the mysterious world of the rainforest.

CHAPTER 61

The Letter

On a cold January night, Marilyn and Larry lounged on the couch, enjoying the warmth from the flames crackling over the logs in the stone fireplace. The dogs lay near the hearth while their newest member, Buddy, rested his muzzle on Larry's lap.

Zachary's mother glanced at the open envelope lying on the coffee table.

"Read it again," Larry requested.

She reached over, tenderly taking out the letter, reading it aloud, "Dear Mom and Dad, I found Conchita! We will be married! Wish you luck on the farm. Love, Zachary."

Marilyn cried, pressing her face into her husband's chest. He tried to comfort her, saying, "He's safe and happy. That's all a parent can hope for, and look on the bright side, he'll be bilingual and a father soon!"

His words upset Marilyn even more. She sobbed, "I may never see my grandkids!" After a while, she calmed down, peering at her husband with cheeks glistening from tears. "At least he's happy. He's probably hunting game and hanging from trees. What more could a boy ask for?"

With a bit of wistfulness, Larry whispered, "Indeed."

About the Author

Shaman Elizabeth Herrera is a healer and author who writes stories that encourage people to stretch outside their comfort zones and reexamine their own beliefs.

She inherited her rebellious spirit from her father who was raised by his grandfather—a full-blooded Apache who smuggled sugar and flour from Mexico into Texas, exchanged gunfire with Texas Rangers and crossed paths with Pancho Villa.

Elizabeth was raised in a Christian home, but lost her faith in her early twenties. For over a decade, she searched for something to fill the void and eventually discovered Native American spirituality (shamanism). Through this spiritual practice, she unexpectedly became a catalyst for healing and miracles. These events led her back to a belief in a higher power.

Elizabeth is the author of the books *Shaman Stone Soup* (Memoir, Inspirational), and *Of Stars and Clay* (Science Fiction/Genetic Engineering/Dystopian, Speculative Fiction, 2017), and *Dreams of Heaven* (Inspirational Fiction, 2017).

To keep abreast of her latest releases, visit ShamanElizabethHerrera.com.

Lightning Source UK Ltd.
Milton Keynes UK
UKHW010620120120
356778UK00001B/152/P